The Floating Order

Order

Erin Pringle

TWO RAVENS
P R E S S

Published by Two Ravens Press Ltd.
Green Willow Croft
Rhiroy
Lochbroom
Ullapool
Ross-shire IV23 2SF

www.tworavenspress.com

The right of Erin Pringle to be identified as author of this work has been asserted by her in accordance with the Copyright, Designs and Patent Act, 1988. © Erin Pringle, 2009.

ISBN: 978-1-906120-42-9

British Library Cataloguing in Publication Data: a CIP record for this book can be obtained from the British Library.

Designed and typeset in Sabon by Two Ravens Press.
Cover photograph © Cindy Pringle.
Cover design by David Knowles and Sharon Blackie.

Printed on Forest Stewardship Council-accredited paper by the MPG books group.

Mixed Sources
Product group from well-managed forests, controlled sources and recycled wood or fiber
www.fsc.org Cert no. TT-COC-002303
© 1996 Forest Stewardship Council
FSC

About the Author

Originally from the Midwest, Erin Pringle has an MFA in Creative Writing from Texas State University. Erin's work has been widely anthologised. Her fiction has been nominated for a Pushcart Prize, named a 'Best American Notable Non-required Reading of 2007', and was short-listed for the 2007 Charles Pick Fellowship.

For more information about the author, see
www.tworavenspress.com

Acknowledgements

The Floating Order stories have appeared in various forms in the following publications:

Electric Velocipede, Adirondack Review, Whistling Shade, The Circle Magazine, Dark Recesses, Pagitica in Toronto, Big Pulp, SUB-LIT, Austin Chronicle, Barrelhouse, Lake Effect, Snowvigate, The Project for a New Mythology, Etchings, Interbirth, Quarter After Eight, Not Normal III, pacificREVIEW, and Porcupine Literary Arts Magazine.

Contents

Wynken and Blynken are two little eyes,
And Nod is a little head,
And the wooden shoe that sailed the skies
Is a wee one's trundle-bed.
So shut your eyes while mother sings
Of wonderful sights that be,
And you shall see the beautiful things
As you rock in the misty sea,
Where the old shoe rocked the fishermen three:
Wynken,
Blynken,
And Nod.

— from *Wynken, Blynken, and Nod*
by Eugene Field

The Floating Order

They say methodical. One by one in the bathtub. They say methodical therefore guilty.

I save my babies in the morning. The sky very blue that morning. Like tiny hands smearing rivers down walls. The bathroom walls are too white. Whiter than the place my husband puts me when I'm not a perfect wife.

Some of my babies' pictures hang on my walls – that's my favorite the house the birds the sky but not the sky that morning or the sky now. The sky now raining rain I have to stare at the razor fence to see.

Someday, I will write a book. I have been contacted. I will start with Wynken, Blynken, and Nod and end with my sad husband and a bible quote. There are so many to choose from.

They have many words. Delusions, psychotic hallucinations, voices.

I have many words. Ghosts, nightmares, friends.

The problem is no one explains until too late that they don't hear them. You say your imaginary friend is biting your arms, and they laugh, pat your pigtails. You show them the marks, and they say don't do that to yourself, or you'll get lockjaw. So you shut up about it. You grow up thinking this is how life is until that friend introduces you to Natalie who introduces you to Ruby. You think everyone needs friends. So you let them push you in the tire swing. You give them your baby-dolls to play with. Then they're holding your flowers and you're saying I do, and everyone says congratulations it's a boy it's a boy but then Ruby introduces you to Pete and they all tell sad stories that make you clutch hard and everyone misunderstands, holds your hands and puts you in a room with lonely people who suck pills.

I made a book for each baby. They are on the top shelf

for when they get older. Their pacifiers didn't fit so they're in a jewelry box on the dresser. My daughter still asks for her binkie, but I pretend I can't hear so she'll give up. Pacifiers ruin babies' mouths.

I am not like those lonely people in the white rooms, which is why I never needed pills. I was not like those lonely people. They tarnished their bodies, their temples. That's why God poured alizarin-crimson paint down the walls so everyone would think it was blood, see their evil ways, and repent the pills out of the nurses' hands. The nurses pretended not to feel the blood trickling from their eyes.

People will buy my book because people always want true stories. They want yes and no. They want people to ask what they're reading. And reading is the only way people will listen to me.

My mother was a schoolteacher. She resigned so she could help take care of my babies. When I was little, she read books to me. She let me smell the pages. My favorite was about a girl made of patches who lived in a faraway land. I copied one of the illustrations and gave my picture of the illustration to my mother for her birthday. She said I had talent, so I copied all the illustrations. She hung them in frames around my bedroom. I thought I'd be an artist.

The doctors asked me to draw pictures. They asked me what they were. I said can't you see? I'm no cubist. They didn't say anything about talent.

I know good and bad, which is why I clutched my legs to keep from hearing my friends' sad stories. They said write down our stories. I yelled 10,000 may fall! They said want to know what your sad story will be? Sad or bad? they asked each other. Sad or bad? My fingers ripped rivers up my legs, but I was good and didn't listen for a long time. My mother was a schoolteacher, my father a preacher. That's why I knew good and bad. They said your babies will be the main characters. I yelled pestilence! They said don't worry, we'll tell you what to do. I clutched hard to keep from following their directions.

I try to be a good girl. In school, I always raised my hand before answering. I could include my grade-cards in my book. Then everyone can see that my behavior was always satisfactory.

I graduated. I sent my art far away. No one liked it. I got married. I had babies.

That's normal.

That won't seem realistic, my agent says.

That's normal, too.

Sometimes, my friends play show-and-tell. Natalie shows her dead child. Alice pets a white goat. Ruby says death is quiet. Pete cradles a large doll. Then they show Father dropping sinners in Lake Michigan. Father crying and dipping my head in the sink. This is how sinners are saved. They show my babies floating on a wide river.

The Mississippi River changed course because the Chicago people didn't want to smell their waste. People shouldn't change nature. God burned down that city. Twice.

My babies' hospital pictures are on the first page. Their tiny hospital bracelets on the second page. Each book has the same format so they won't get jealous and argue. I hate conflict.

When my friends show pictures of my babies floating, I clutch hard until the picture vanishes like rain. Rain goes into the ground then returns to the sky. Like babies.

My sister is a photographer. When she visits, she holds pictures up to the glass that separates us. When we were little, she was always taking pictures. If she ran out of ideas, she took pictures of us. We are always blurry because her arms weren't long enough to keep us at the right distance. You have to snap at the right distance. There aren't any pictures of our brother. Probably because he's the youngest so everyone was tired of taking pictures by then. If you've seen one baby you've seen them all.

If you've seen one horror movie. If you've read one birthday

3

card.

My sister took slides of my paintings so I could send a portfolio to the art colleges. They didn't think I had talent.

My daughter walked before her brothers did, but I wrote that she walked at the same time, so they wouldn't think God played favorites. I let the liquid out of their teething rings and pasted them in the middle of the books.

God moved water for Moses. There must have been fish flopping. He must have seen their gills rippling too fast.

You have to hold a camera at least three feet away for there to be a focus.

My babies opened and shut their mouths.

The bad man showed the reel of my babies so happy reciting Wynken, Blynken, and Nod. Their loving eyes in the camera. My mother sat behind me and cried. My husband didn't make a sound. My brother cartwheeled across the courtroom, his shadow on the screen. No one saw those babies' sins and how to hell forever flaming if not saved.

If my father weren't dead, he would have told the bad man let her talk. Explain how she read her bible every day. How she illustrated her favorite stories.

When I was scared of the dark and screamed, he rushed in. He read me Psalms. 10,000 may fall. Do not fear the pestilence that stalks. Arrows by day.

Let her talk!

He said repeat these words until stuck in your head. If your imaginary friends won't listen, say them louder. Yell if you have to. If your mom's home, take a bath and scream the words underwater. I remembered the words for a long time. The pills made me forget.

My eldest has nightmares. He sneaks in our bedroom and crawls between my husband and me. He's a good child most of the time. He calls his brother and sister his babies. He'll be a fine father. Any girl would be lucky. I was also a loving child. I knew everyone's birthdays, I sent my drawings to my grandparents. Both sets. I made Christmas presents. Painted ornaments. My children are the same.

In the middle of my book will be my wedding pictures my sister took. The orange blossoms. Me in my white dress. On my father's arm. On my husband's. The bouquet on its way down into my sister's hands. She must not have taken that one. My brother was not invited. When the preacher or judge asked if anyone had words to say she said she dug her hands into her legs to avoid yelling I OBJECT – SHE'S AN ARTIST! She pasted the wedding pictures into a genuine leather album.

There are so many pictures it might be a good idea just to publish all my albums. I must ask my agent.

My daughter's hair is blonde. So soft. It will darken as she grows older. Boys will go wild over her. My husband will ask what their intentions are. Boys with tattoos won't make it through the front door because every body is a temple.

I cheek the pills. I drool the sour onto my shirt cuff and spit when no one's looking. The nurses say bad girl to do so. The red paint patterns their faces into lace, into paper doilies for valentines. I close my eyes and say my mother's a school-teacher and will make them stand against the chalkboard. My brother agrees with the nurses. He's a lady-chaser. He hugs them from behind, his hands on their breasts. The problem is sometimes my brother is a joker, and sometimes he looks out for me. But when he says listen to the nurses, I don't. That is reverse psychology.

One of my youngest sons is musical and will be a concert pianist like his father should have been.

Once a month, my husband and I are allowed to hug, hold hands. He has strong hands. The last time he didn't wear his wedding ring. I didn't say anything. We're still married, though, but no babies. My husband wants a barrel full of children. I might want some one day, but my career is first priority.

He counts the pills, wraps my fingers over them with his strong hands. His hands are strong from playing the piano every day. Please, he says. Please for the children. Our favorite song is Mozart's *Sonata in C Major*. He doesn't understand that when babies grow they disobey. The children run around the living room when he plays.

Honor thy parents is a commandment.

There are many scales in that sonata.

So fast.

Why wasn't he wearing his ring?

Moses' mother floated him away from her. She meant well.

I asked my mother about giving birth, but she didn't remember. That was back when they knocked everyone out. So when she woke up they handed me to her, and she thought, is this my baby? Everybody says it hurts, but it's worth it. That's not very vivid. One woman said if everybody knew the truth no one would have children. Then why do so many have more than one? I thought.

The problem is you have to know what questions to ask to get the right answers, but because I'd never had a baby, I didn't know to ask if it was like the monthly cramps that crippled me to the bathroom floor. If it was like twelve months of cramps all in one day.

My husband's strong hands clench and unclench when we talk on the telephones connected by the glass my sister holds her pictures against. My sister says the buzz in the line means tapping. That the guards record my words to use against me. This is part of the guilty torture. She says at night the moans in the pipes are my recorded voice played slow. I tried to explain what she said to my husband, but he said I don't have a sister. They don't have a good relationship. She thought I could do better. She said how can you be an artist if you're married? I reminded her that the art colleges didn't think I had talent. He doesn't like her because of the stories. Like when she pushed

6

me down a hot slide. She said if I slid fast enough, I'd fly out of the park and right up to God. Then I could apologize for the evil thoughts.

The problem is sometimes God's mean, and sometimes he's not.

The slide burned the bottoms of my thighs. My mother smeared aloe vera on them. She kept the aloe vera in a jam jar in the refrigerator so it'd be cool and soothing.

My agent says a whole chapter should explain crazy. Everyone misunderstands. I did. They say crazy is muddled. If I'm crazy, this isn't true. My friends' words are clear. Not blah blah blah but do this and this and this. That morning it was save them save them save them. Very clear. Like an empty church and then one voice. Then two. I sang in the church choir when I was little. My robe was white and went to my knees. I always wished it went past my calves like my mother's. She still sings in the choir.

The man behind the big desk wore a robe, but it was black. My brother climbed on the desk and pulled his mouth wide and stuck out his tongues so I'd laugh. He always wants to be the center of attention because he's youngest.

All my friends were there. They sat in the box with the people whose eyes slithered around me.

They asked why I didn't like them anymore. They said come play with us. We miss you. Sad or bad? Sad or bad?

People use the word crazy too loosely. They throw it around. They are careless with words.

I've tried to end the friendships. On our honeymoon, I asked my husband to squeeze my head with his very strong hands. Squeeze and squeeze. He refused. He clutched me tight and said I'll never hurt you. He didn't understand, and I couldn't explain because he wouldn't love me anymore.

I wonder who got into those art colleges. I wonder what those colleges did with my slides. They didn't send them back. My sister said maybe they copied the slides to make your paintings look like their paintings then destroyed yours and sold theirs. How can you know? How can you prove that it's your art since you sold your paintings to buy your wedding dress?

I asked the policeman if he'd like some juice, as we were out of milk. He was polite. I explained that my babies are saved. He held my hand and opened the car door for me. Natalie sat in the passenger seat and played with the radio dials. I told her to stop it. The policeman asked who I was talking to. I wouldn't explain. My husband has such high hopes.

After they drove me away from the morning, they locked me naked under a rainless roof. Then they clothed me and sat me in a tiny room at a table. People with clipboards came in and asked questions. Why bother I wondered since I'd already told the policeman my babies were saved. I wanted to be good and explain, but the words clogged. Like typewriter ribbon in a small drain. You can see the inky black words, but they're shoved tight so you pull and pull to read them aloud, but everyone thinks you're shy or stupid because no sound comes out. They said just answer yes or no. But their questions never had one answer. They asked my babies' ages, but they were never one age.

Just answer.

My husband is very convincing. He could have been a lawyer or an exorcist. It's nice to be led sometimes. We had a puppy when we first married. I loved it. But sometimes I couldn't handle it. Especially when my husband wasn't there. It never greeted me after I opened the door and saw the library book shredded on the floor. A hardcover, no less. There really was no thought. I opened the door – shredded book – heat surges through me – I scream – I hit. I wept. Gave it handfuls of treats. I avoided the library. Overdue notices in the mailbox, automated messages on the answering machine. Finally, I took the shreds to the library and my checkbook and apologized to the librarian and told her I wasn't that kind of person and

I wept and she said it's okay and I wrote the check crying, wiping my nose then realized I was using her pen and my snot was on it and she saw the snot on my hand and on the pen so I purposely slid the pen into my checkbook in an accidental way. I should have washed it and brought it back or bought them a pack of pens, but then I'd have to explain why and then I'd probably cry again. It's hard to stop unexpected tears because you're trying to quit but realizing why and so crying harder. My husband said it was just a library book, and you paid for it. But what if someone had checked out that book every year and when she went to check it out there was a new copy? Then she'd feel loss and think an irresponsible person with no reverence for the borrowing system caused the damage. But I do have reverence. My mother let me smell the pages.

My daughter has fair skin like me. The boys are dark like their father. My husband is so handsome, especially when the light over the sheet music plays across his face, plays his face into love, into concentration, into what he is when he's not paying attention. Like walking by a mirror without realizing it.

Someday, I will get those files about me. I will photocopy them for my book. Everyone will see how they tried to fool me. Everyone will understand crazy by then and call the doctors. They will say read her book. They will say malpractice.

The two oldest can count. One to forever and one to twenty.

I babysat as a teenager. I told my mother I don't want children. She said it will be different when they're your own.

I will teach home-ec when my daughter is in high school. When I was in high school, the teacher gave each of us an egg in a napkin, but it was no crying-vomiting-mommy-mommy baby. She didn't explain that there's no guarantee you'll love it the first time in your arms. That you may think what is this wriggling thing. But you learn. And the baby becomes

9

your only. You will hurt yourself to save it. I tried to, but my husband cut the rope with his strong hands. He couldn't save me. I said Judas had a rope. He said you're not Judas. I said that's not the point.

They asked over clipboards if I remembered this. I said only his tired eyes. Yes or no they demanded.

They said you planned it. Yes or no. They said you knew to float this baby before that one. Three follows two follows one. They said you were methodical. I asked if alphabetical order was methodical. Yes or no they said.

My husband or I suggested another baby.

My sister said you have two or three already. She said what happened to your talent? What about the gallery we're going to open?

I said a man's seed should not be wasted on dry earth. Plus his eyes can be happy again. Plus my friends always go on vacation when I'm pregnant. I stopped the birth control and pills. This was good because babies are hurt when bad's in the blood.

And my blood was bad which is why Father dunked me and why I needed to fly to God and why I hid the rope on the top shelf.

The problem is lots of women think like me but they don't say it out loud. Even about basic things like breasts. Like when my husband sucked at my nipples and I'd think about a baby being there. I'd imagine his head a baby's head and then I'd want to throw up. I'd worry that when I had a baby I'd imagine it to be my husband's head until I got used to it and then what would it be like when my husband's balding head moved under the covers again?

My sister said there's another woman he visits when you are cheeking and drooling. She said that's why sometimes the babies look like only him and a beautiful woman. His other woman birthed your babies. All your ultrasounds were prerecorded and the pill the doctors said would give you a healthy mother's body was really like one of those pills that you drop in the sink and it expands into a foam dinosaur the size of your hand. You were always so gullible.

If your babies hear voices, clutch them tight and yell. Recite *Wynken, Blynken, and Nod* until they fall asleep. Sing and sing so they will always hear your voice over the others. I liked it when Mom sang in the choir. All the voices blending, but I could hear hers because I knew it.

It is wrong to judge what God hasn't judged. But they did.

It is wrong to float babies, they said.

The bad man pointed at me and said what woman would give life and take it away?

I did not see one in the courtroom.

Many mothers have children and a mental illness and you don't see them drowning.

But they are, I said. They just clutch better than I could.

My brother applauded.

I raised my hand so they'd let me talk.

Hand down, my lawyer said.

But the sky my babies smeared it like sinners.

The sky, my lawyer said, is unnecessary because if you are crazy you don't notice things like blue or bad.

My sister: I told you not to have children.

My husband: You weren't bad, you were ill.

I am not ill, I told him.

His hands held tired eyes.

If I had a picture of this, I wouldn't put it in the book. How it shatters me.

I will say that words are babies, you must correct their sins or the evil takes over and they float away. I will try to explain how their eyelashes fluttered against mine every night. I will write a chapter about each one. The father, the musician, the looker.

I think I would have been happier being a bag boy at

the grocery store. Helping old ladies out with their groceries. Living alone. Having food only I liked in the house. One fork, one spoon, one knife, one teacup, one pot, one baking sheet. Just one of everything. A bicycle. Bicycling to the park on dark days and sitting on the slide or merry-go-round and just thinking. Maybe saving up enough money to visit places with beautiful names that shape your mouth like the word chocolate or possible. I'd eat in small cafés by the window.

Maybe I'd have a cat. One with three legs. Cats think about eating you. If you become the person to die alone in your easy chair, it doesn't take much time before they abandon the dinner bowl for your skin. All cats will turn feral if left alone in a matter of days. Feral is a lovely word. I'd like a visiting cat. One I'd buy cat food for but never name because it's someone else's. We had a cat growing up.

We ate Cheerios. I took my pills. My sister ran the water and tested if it was too hot. My husband drove to get milk. Skim milk is healthiest for babies. After one is done floating, I call another. My voice echoes in the bathroom, tub full of water the bottom stuck with sticky flowers to avoid slipping. My babies' arms flapping as if to swim to fly. I tell them float. Don't think just float. I lullaby them into floating. Their mouths opening and shutting. Their hair webbing above flowers.

My babies love me, and I love them. Their innocence will save them and they'll be far from this world that judges without God and the world that burns without God. I recite *Wynken, Blynken, and Nod* while toweling them dry.

How they'll sail.

I'll never stop clutching.

Cats and Dogs

Mom's coming home because rain means storm walk. Because it rains dads and moms. Mom will fall from a cloud and into the pond, a horse trough, the roof – daisied dress catching in eaves. But Fannie won't know when.

If Mom falls on the roof, Fannie must be there to swoop up and take her hand. So Mom won't hurt herself or slip, Fannie will point out loose nails, scattered tree branches. Any storm walk could be the one, even if Fannie's brother Deddy says no.

It's gonna rain dads and moms, Deddy.

No, Fannie, cats and dogs.

No matter how many times Fannie bends her knees, flattens her feet and pushes the bunk mattress above her where Deddy sleeps, Deddy will not agree Mom will fall. Deddy will not even say it rains dads and moms. He's so convincing, Fannie sometimes wonders if Mom existed.

No matter how many droughts or how many times Deddy says it's cats and dogs not dads and moms, a storm will roll in. All greens will intensify. The gray porch whitens. The wind chimes clring clring. And Fannie stormwalks down the gravel path to mother, her palms raised and catching the droplets. Like in the good dreams.

Not like in the dreams where Fannie and Dad sit out on the dock fishing with a bag of cats instead of worms. He ties each cat around the neck and tosses it out into the water but nothing's biting. Soon there's a tug on Fannie's line. Dad gets behind her and holds the rod, saying hold tight – lean back – keep your weight low. The fishing rod bridges.

First, the hair rises.

Then the forehead.

The throat necklaced with moss, eye sockets emptying minnows.

13

And Fannie wakes up screaming, kicking off the covers. Deddy moans.

Their dad's in prison for killing his dad. Murder, one house says. Self-defense, another says.

Their dad doesn't know about the men who visited his house five counties away. The men who replaced faucets, tightened hinges, and disappeared into his wife's bedroom while his son was at school and his daughter was in her playpen, standing still. And he doesn't know his wife should fall from the clouds any day now.

Now that Fannie and Deddy are the only ones left, Fannie promises to call Deddy by his real name, Tom, but her head won't cooperate. Like her legs when it rains. Fannie's first word was Deddy. Afraid Fannie'd stop saying it before they visited Father, Mom called Tom Deddy so Fannie wouldn't forget the sound of daddy while hers was in prison.

Deddy commands Fannie to stay put or else, but Fannie can't stay put. Because rain.

Because even when she was a promise inside Mom, feet flat and pushing, Mom walked up and down the red path to quiet her. And when Mom couldn't sleep, she strapped Fannie to her chest and walked. Once Fannie began toddling – every sharp edge a foreseeable disaster – Mom buckled her in the stroller and pushed her up and down the path, wheels puffing dust.

Sometimes, Fannie sits in the stroller even though she's too big. Once she asked Deddy to push her. The stroller was gone the next day.

Stay put is out of the question.

Deddy chases after Fannie because no one knows Mom's gone. When the town finds out, they'll mow over the sunflowers, drown the cats, empty the house and auction everything off. Every umbrella to the highest bidder. The bunk bed will go to another house, for other kids, but the bottom kid won't know to press her feet against the mattress above her to get her brother's attention. The town will send Deddy and Fannie to new parents who make them wear shoes and play inside when it rains.

The first time Fannie stormwalked, Deddy didn't find her until almost dark, storm wrung to drizzle. Out at Riggin's pond. Her tiny body hunched at the end of the teetering dock, feet swimming shadows over the water.

Whatchya doin', sis?

She didn't look up, dirty cheeks lined with tears or rain.

Fannie?

She might land here. She can't swim. Gonna rescue her.

Who? he asked.

Mom.

She ain't coming. Come on home, he said, pulling Fannie up by her armpits.

She kneed his ribs, punched his face to blood until he looked like the evening sky when he had come home late from school during Dad's trial. Mom sat on the porch swing – Fannie in her lap – the both of them watching Deddy dawdle down the path and to the porch stair. Mom waited for him not to speak before she asked what had happened – Fight?

Deddy's knuckles bled as he stroked the yellow tom at his leg.

Fannie gurgled, throwing her baby weight against her mother's arms. Mom leaned back in the porch swing.

The cat was missing half an ear, bald patches dotted its fur.

Mom closed her eyes. She said in that cat's younger days, he got in some pretty bad fights. Gone days at a time. Once, some cat tore into him so bad you couldn't tell his real color. If that cat could speak, we'd spend three days talking back to front before his story's told.

Deddy slumped against her leg, lip swollen. What's a murderer? he asked.

Mom opened her eyes.

15

The day Mom leaves, she awakes and thinks it's raining inside. In one bedroom, Fannie struggles to snap up her red slicker for their walk. In the other, water crashes around Mom, seeping into the closet, filling it up, and dirtying all the clothes. *Even once the house dries, there will still be mildew, and even bleach will not stop the mildew weaving into stationery and he'll smell it on my handwriting, it will fill his cell. If he ever comes home, he'll see the wilting walls and turn with the disappointment of all these years on his face and ask why.* When she closes and opens her eyes, the rain stays put outside her bedroom window.

She blinks.

Again the rain flows inside. Yesterday's dress floats by. The ceiling bows. If she can find one or two umbrellas, she can climb onto the roof and plug the hole.

She opens her eyes.

The roof peels and thuds against the outside wall. The rain pins her to the mattress, spills into her eyes, ears, sloshes in the room's corners.

Fannie finds Mom in the bedroom, legs poking from beneath bed, arms sweeping. Dust angel.

Time to Storm Walk, Mom.

Rain, rain, go away, Mom whispers, her eyes far and away.

Mom hurries past her. Into the kitchen. She flings open the cabinets, stoops beneath the sink. Into the living room and she's turning. Ballerina in jewelry box. Fannie goes to her, arms out. Mom cups Fannie's chin, fingertips grazing Fannie's hairline. I'll find it, child, she says then steps off the porch, the wind lifting her skirt – a pattern of spilled daisies – above the backs of her knees. The rain slants right to left.

The front door is gone now. A square white space on the porch where the welcome mat once lay beneath a napping cat. Now, cats shotgun through the house. Now, Deddy won't touch them. He remembers when the house smelled of fresh paint. When water faucets gleamed and all doors swung straight. If Mom does fall, which she won't – but if she does, he will lift Fannie onto his shoulders so she can reach to take Mom's hand like a water droplet. They'll carry Mom home and lay her in the bathtub, rinse her hair and towel her dry. Then he'll quit his job at the mechanics, go back to school, and Fannie will stay put. He'll be too old to lean against Mom's leg as she tugs the cow's udders, but the cats' whiskers will drip milk.

When Dad bought the land, Mom made a picnic. Dad promised Tom a swimming hole. He pointed. A kitchen here, a hallway there, vegetable and flower gardens. His hands made a camera and took pictures of his young wife's face. He ran around the invisible foundation. Climbed pretend stairs. They laughed and ate chicken and deviled eggs, apple pie. Mom smiled down at Dad's head on her pregnant headrest. A red barn this big – his hands outstretched – and a Betsy cow for milk and butter. Tom napped under a future clothesline. Every passing cloud a flapping sheet.

The mechanic watches Deddy watch storm. On storm days, he lets Deddy leave early. The boy wants to play in the rain and it's the least he can do, like giving him the job even though he's not of age. If Deddy brings money home, it might keep Deddy's mom from letting men into the house. The mechanic tilts his head to the deepening dark. It's a shame how it all turned out.

Deddy is at school when Mom wakes to the drowning house. He carefully copies the teacher's handwriting from the board onto his chalkboard as Fannie stands in the kitchen archway and Mom spreads herself on the kitchen floor that she thinks is the roof – over a leak that isn't there – palms flat on linoleum. Maybe she can swallow all the rain before it ruins her whole life. Maybe the roof will spin off, and she'll ride it to the prison, and she and the only man she's loved will fly to the mountains to the lake where they met. He swam across the lake to where she floated on a raft in a white bikini. How long ago that was.

Don't storm walk into the steelyard, Deddy warns Fannie.

How come?

Mom won't land there.

Just 'cause you're five fingers older than me don't mean you know nothing about nothing.

Look here, Fannie, the steelyard is the last place in the world she'd fall. If she did fall. Which she won't. It's shut down, dangerous.

It will rain dads and moms!

Seeing as how I'm the man of the house now and I say for you to not go there, then don't. Asides, I won't look there to save you if you go and hurt yourself. You hear me, Fannie?

It will. I know it will.

Deddy thumps her feet from the mattress.

Just before Dad drove up the red path and to the sheriff's office, he pulled aside Tom, Fannie murmuring in his arms.

Go to the steelyard to remember, son.

What, Deddy doesn't know.

Go to the steelyard to remember, son, Dad said again when the judge said For Life.

Deddy still isn't sure, but he goes anyway. Maybe one day while sitting on the old barrel where Dad took cigarette breaks when the heat was too much and the steel rippled like a pond, Deddy will remember whatever *it* is. And when Dad comes home and says, Son, did you remember like I asked, Deddy – who will be Tom again – will nod, and Dad will shake his hand, and they'll dig a swimming hole. They'll sweat and spit.

And Fannie will be Dad's job again.

Deddy doesn't know how, on dry days, Fannie sneaks to the houses in town. She climbs through windows and finds the umbrellas – always kept in front-room closets or vases beside doors. No one knows the umbrella is missing until clouds churn across the sky.

Sometimes, Fannie overhears conversations in the houses. Usually, they're about a church bazaar or grandchildren or whose marriage is still falling apart. But she has heard her own name and frozen.

The house with the blue polka-dotted umbrella says her father killed her grandfather in a fit of rage. Of course, he was in a rage. So what? Think about it. Why would Senior even be at their house at that time of day? Why would he do that to his daughter-in-law? Regardless, we must remember that at the bottom of all this are those odd children.

As the woman lay on the linoleum, she remembers being a little girl under her mother's umbrella – pink striped, white ruffle – how safe she was back then as a young girl not yet on the path to becoming a mother with her own umbrella. *She probably still has it. Must go fast now, or too late and the house ruined.*

A little girl chases after her, calling her mom, asking where she's going to – can I come, too – storms – walks –

Go home, child. Go home to your mother and stay put.

Why can't I come?

You must wait for your mother. You must wait and she will let you stand beneath her umbrella.

The girl tugs at the woman's dress, her fingers pinching the hem where a daisy disappears into the seam. Her cheeks washed by confusion and rain.

As soon as Mom finds the umbrella or gives up and returns, Fannie will be there, her face a sunflower. Dad promised Mom and little Tom so many sunflowers. Alone, shirt off, and spread on future foundation, he dreamt of Tom swinging on a rope into the swimming hole, of Fannie dancing in the living room.

Hey, Deddy.

Go to sleep.

19

Smell it?

Hush. I gotta work early.

My legs are tingling, Deddy. A storm, Deddy. It'll storm hard. And we'll wake to it. Right, Deddy? And we can splash in puddles when you get home. That'll be grand. Right, Deddy? My legs say it's gonna rain in the mornin' and so maybe Mom will come home. And she and me will hold hands.

And walk down the dirt path into town like they used to.

Past the widows rocking on porches. Past the leering barbershop men, old friends of Grandfather.

Fannie licked the stamp and sent the envelope with the letter to Dad Out of Town. She knew as soon as it left her hand, it appeared in Dad's, and he kissed the letter where Mom and she had and where Deddy would've if he weren't so stubborn. Dad's letters never came quick enough. Mom read them for bedtime stories. Deddy turned to the wall, pretending not to hear.

Fannie forgives Deddy for not letting her see what's in the cigar box on the shelf above his pillow. She knows Dad's gun is in there. She hasn't told him she knows because he doesn't know about her umbrellas or how she worries Mom might not come back. Because maybe Mom's found Dad, and they can't remember how to get home.

Maybe while Deddy was at work and she was borrowing umbrellas, they did come back, and they saw the house, and one of the cats hobbled by, belly thin and throat too dry to meow, so they hid their eyes and ran away to build a new house and have babies worth staying around for.

The house with blue umbrellas says the steelyard is an eyesore. But what can be done if Senior's dead and Junior's in prison and the boy's only ten? Junior's lawyer said no evidence. Believe what you will. Doesn't history repeat? Doesn't that family prove it?

Hey, Deddy. What was Dad like?

Deddy snores.

She kicks his mattress again. Deddy, you remember Dad?

He snores louder.

I don't remember him, Deddy, so do you? Do you? You remember. You need to tell me what he was like.

Deddy snores until she's crying and pulling herself up into his bunk. Slapping and pinching his face.

Tell me!

Still he snores.

The trailer with a child's rainbow-striped umbrella says maybe Junior's wife was the one who actually tore up the house instead of Senior. Maybe she called Senior to come over because she needed his help before Junior came home. Maybe when Senior came over and saw what she had done and realized how disappointed Junior would be – you know how hard he worked on that house – he told her just that and she started ripping down the curtains and what Junior's lawyer said was an attack was actually Senior holding her back in an effort to protect the house. You know that woman. You remember what she did in third-grade just as well as I do. Just like that son of hers.

Something's wrong in his eyes. They dart to the sky and back at you.

Sky and you.

The house with three black umbrellas says Junior shouldn't have turned himself in. His family – such a nice family – could've met him somewhere. Canada. No one would've known the difference. It was self-defense just like his lawyer said.

But when the state wants blood.

Of course, Fannie storm searches the steelyard because even if that's the last place in the world, Mom could fall there by accident – the wind pushing her off course.

Fannie slithers under the fence; it catches her wet hair and dress. For a second she thinks she's stuck and will die there, half in, and the last image will be her mother's yellow sundress and muddied calves drifting down. Fannie breaks free, hair and fabric left in the wire. She wanders, touching the rusty pipes. The smell here is the same as the cigar box and Dad's flannel shirt hidden under Deddy's pillow. Fannie hears tears. She follows them to the shed.

She crawls through a hole in the base of the building. Rain drips onto a hunched figure.

Dad.

When he turns, Fannie will run to him. He'll catch her up and kiss her hard. They'll go to the pond, and Mom will be there, floating on her back, hands propelling her in lazy circles. Deddy will jump in the water and splash around with a huge smile.

But it's not Dad.

It's Deddy sitting on a barrel and shaking.

All of Fannie's umbrellas open and surrounding his feet.

Fannie looks at her legs. She looks at the umbrellas.

Cats and dogs, Deddy, she says.

Cats and dogs, Tom.

Looker

Understand your mother and I drove three hours. We got up early after sleeping poorly then on the road. She wanted to stop, snap a picture of a stand that sold pumpkins palm trees pecans, but I'd forgotten the camera. Plus we were tired. We lounged naked a hot month to afford the tickets, so we kept the windows open, but the upstairs neighbors yelled. Your mother's leg thrown over my back.

Outside the concert a woman with a whistle sat on a horse by a pond. Moss in that pond not like the condoms in the river.

Today on smoke break, I counted ten condoms in the river. Think if I'd stood there for half an hour. An hour. If I were still there how many condoms.

Understand your mother wore vanilla perfume on her wrists her neck beneath her knees.

Two hours.

Understand she was a looker. You've seen pictures. The one of her in a green bathing suit holding a cigarette over the kitchen sink. Doris Day your grandmother called her.

Understand that night definitely she wore a yellow tube top. Believe me it was tight and I could tell no bra because she was excited why wouldn't she be. The AC off all month to afford tickets. We bought generic and turned lights off in rooms we weren't in. We lounged while neighbors argued about babies. The wife wanted the husband didn't. Your mother wanted to pet the horse's nose but didn't.

Back then your mother wore perfume I liked. Back when she was a looker and stood at sinks in bathing suits.

We hadn't gone out alone for a month – my hands on the wheel her feet waving out the window at people we sped by. She saw things your mother. She saw cigarette smokers in drivers' seats. She'd watch peripheral because directly would

23

make them turn.

We didn't take a blanket. She thought maybe maybe not. Why bother she decided, and when we were on the lawn, everyone with tickets lounged on blankets, as if in their own backyards. Not many had yards your mother assured me.

The balcony neighbors drank wine then bickered. Maybe their names were Cheryl and Dick. When we moved in they invited us up your mother said why not so we brought a bottle of wine because that's what you do.

Understand your mother knew what was what.

When the concert began everyone stood on the blankets so what's the point she said. The horse's nose was white and brown and breathed on my arm when I walked by. Your mother wanted but didn't.

Your mother was a sleeptalker. In the mornings I'd tell her what she'd said then she'd laugh, kiss my ear.

I held her belt loops during the slow songs. She rested her chin on my neck or scratched between my shoulder blades.

We have no pictures of the little stand under a thatched roof and palm trees. The sign's paint dried mid-drip: PALM TREES PECANS PUMPKINS.

Ten condoms in five minutes can you believe it?

At the concert she couldn't find her cigarette lighter, so when people held theirs in the air, she turned to the boy behind us with an unlit in her mouth.

Your grandmother was wrong about Doris Day. More like Janis Joplin without freckles.

During fast songs she bumped against me because her body couldn't control the music – her hips swinging – hair all over. Everyone else stood. Everyone else stoic. Ten thousand stoics. That many people makes me think death. All these people will have children grow old die maybe tomorrow in a car wreck at a usually safe intersection. Back window blood shards. All these people twenty thirty forty fifty then returning to reunion concerts to relive the experience. But they can't.

Were the condoms all from one couple, or did someone stand at another bridge dropping them in to make me wonder?

Cheryl and Dick immediately opened the wine. They pulled two more chairs on the balcony and we sat circled. They were older and told us what they were like when they were us and visited people like them for wine on balconies.

Back when your mother was a looker we walked naked and survived without blankets.

Your mother shouldn't have smoked.

If I'd remembered the camera then you'd see her bent over the bridge in her yellow tube top squinting over moss into sunset. Or the stoic holding up his lighter and your mother turning with the unlit cigarette between her lips.

Cheryl and Dick toasted advice. Cheryl said always have something you both enjoy. They hiked. They took their weekends to the mountains. Cheryl watercolored flowers. Dick collected leaves. He promised to show me but didn't.

Why did all those concert couples bother hugging since they'd split up in a month a year or marry have a kid and die of pressure in the heart? The kid will take it hard and that absence always with him. Even at concerts.

Cheryl held her wineglass over her heart and said hold every moment dear because there comes a time yes a time.

We didn't understand.

Vanilla and sweat were enough back then. At night your mother sleeptalked thoughts she wouldn't tell me when I could respond. That's how I found out about you.

Your mother wasn't Day or Joplin but someone famous in a foreign country.

If I closed my eyes 10,000 people weren't dying behind hospital mini blinds and there was only her arm brushing mine – vanilla. Understand I forgot the camera, but she forgot the blanket on purpose.

I love you the first time in her sleep. In the morning when

I told her I love you she tapped her fingernails on the counter. Understand she tapped her fingernails when nervous or avoiding.

I don't know what happened to the green bathing suit.

She did not tap about you.

After the wine and balcony your mother said Cheryl and Dick aren't happy. Far from in fact. Your mother made us promise never to have only paintings and leaves. Believe me your mother was. If there'd been a camera.

All those condoms making their way down and me ashing my cigarette in the same river. It made me sick is what it did.

How could everyone stand there with crossed arms I needed to know. Who? your mother asked on the car ride home windows up feet on floorboards.

Maybe she feigned sleep when talking. I was there when her heart stopped talking.

The horse trotted around after the concert. The whistle in the woman's mouth. She stood between the grass and pond and people filing back to parking lots. She said keep off the grass. Order. Order.

I don't know who took the picture of your mother in the kitchen. I don't know what she's saying but her mouth is open maybe laughing because she sees herself as a picture in an album. Saw herself looking through the album at not just you and me but all of us looking.

I don't know what happened to the album.

If it rained and the ground turned to mud then our blanket would be ruined your mother was adamant. Understand she didn't like ruin. The mossy pond the river condoms all those people finding out next week they're pregnant but their heart's watering their lungs.

Understand your mother wanted to pick you up. Understand she couldn't bend over.

Your mother stamped with the drummer. Her whole body

taking in music and giving back. All those people's mailboxes full of hospital bills their pictures on gas station coffee cans because now the windows must be closed.

I held your mother tight and inhaled.

The sign's red paint was your mother's heart mid-drip I know now.

I didn't buy band T-shirts because we'd wear them a while then give them to the thrift store and what's the point of someone wearing our shirts but not understanding how excited your mother was in her yellow tube top and how she knew the horse's nose was soft.

Order! People wouldn't stay off the grass because what's the point in shuffling behind someone behind someone just trusting that someone else knows? Only a few climbed the fence.

If I had bought her a shirt, maybe one day I might have found it at a thrift store, and remember what I don't anymore.

Any day we expected Cheryl down the stairs with a suitcase of watercolors. We didn't sleep well because the heat your mother's leg sweating across my back and our neighbors – baby – I don't want a baby – liar – you promised.

Understand only a few jumped the fence and everyone else died or divorced.

Understand 2,880 condoms if I were still smoking by the river.

Understand your mother's heart became a bass line for a song it didn't recognize. I'm sorry we didn't cross the fence. We were tired. 10,000 mossy faces. The path to the parking lot was through a grove of trees.

I never slept because her words at any moment. I held her wrist. I counted the heartbeats. I sang slow songs in case her pulse would listen. I held my hand above her chest and imagined miracles.

Order on the path!

She saw and turned. She saw trees and pulled me. Believe me I followed.

I don't know who took the picture of her not looking like anyone foreign or famous.

No one only wants faded watercolors discolored leaves but try to understand.

Don't think if your mother never smoked cigarettes. Don't think if she never got sick.

Order on the path.

I'm so sorry she cried in her sleep her arms outstretched I didn't tell her in the morning.

Understand everyone. We didn't. They saw her hold my waist and scratch with her fingernails but everyone forgets cameras and how their backs once felt. They didn't know tapping meant. Believe me her body was a safe intersection without a blanket beneath the trees thatching above us. Her body a picture of yellow music. All was her hands rubbing my jeans her breath vanilla her legs hot around my waist. The vanilla purest in the inch behind her ear. Understand your mother was. We didn't think about balconies or condoms. Your mother was. It wasn't until we were in the car the radio off the windows up that we thought about you. That night her sleeptalk said she knew the very moment. She did not tap about you your mother.

Losing, I Think

The delivery goes well. A scar across my abdomen and stretch marks treading flesh. Mother crosses herself and dangles a rosary – pink and white swirled glass – above my head. It reminds me of when we were kids, and you pushed me into the pond to prove you could save me. Ice ripping and numbing. Breathing out without an in. The punch and paralysis. I whisper your name to our baby – her name is Eleanor because I remember how much you like The Beatles. Or maybe it's me.

Water is my cure for your constant vacation. I can choose the heat and length of its touch. A pool or waterfall. Sometimes, I can't pull myself from its grasp.

We sat by the water's edge – salt stinging the glass cuts beneath my toes, and I wondered if you broke the half-full 7-Up bottle. Green glass like my eyes through the doorknob's pupil.

When you told me how you played in your father's semi-truck as a child, curling in the cab's mix of apple cider and cherry cavendish tobacco, I listened as intently as you stared at the power lines.

You say it is possible to float in the Dead Sea without thinking. The salt still clinging to your jaw as I sucked its sting into my lips, chapped in a world of four seasons.

The blisters were still fresh from raking maple and oak into separate piles. You did not notice my Band-Aids, even though they pressed your palms. I agreed that the tan lines on your feet from the plastic flip-flops were suave. We stuck to the first layer of epidermis.

Your mouth at my breast too close beneath the comforter. Pushing you away with raw hands, I winced, but you didn't notice, busy feeling betrayed.

We danced in the bar. I didn't know the steps. You held me close and looked over my shoulder. I closed my eyes.

Lighthouses are pathetic collectors' items. You laughed, tapping my refrigerator magnets, and left your roll of Nova Scotia scenes on the coffee table while I washed dishes. I drove you to the airport. Again.

As you tipped cocktails with the passenger next to you, I wrote our names on paper. Dipped them in water. Froze them because this was supposed to keep us together. That night I dreamed of witches, of Salem, you watching me burn.

The postcards were late again. I was too. I pasted the store-bought disregard in the scrapbook. It doubled for first steps and words. An aerial view of Prague next to "Sleeps through the night."

I took a ceramics class in Lawrence. Earth tones and wet clay between fingers, filling in lifelines, hope lines. You've been to Greece and Italy and so will be disappointed by my hands.

The sound of you stumbling up my steps with jet-lagged feet. Door left unlatched year round for these rare occasions. I only had leftover liver. Your hands skied my belly-slope. You never used the flash when I insisted on a picture. I knew it wouldn't develop or wrinkle in your wallet. We ordered in lasagna. I told you I was craving. You didn't ask what and left me with aluminum-foil containers clotted with burned cheese.

There was a news report today on the Red Light district in

Amsterdam. I stand in the window nightly. Waiting for the car door slam and footsteps that don't come. Please don't bring me a souvenir.

It's a week before you secede this time. I mourn over iced tea. Sit in the wicker couch on the porch that pokes the soft flesh of the backs of my arms and thighs. More affectionate than your toes in my ears. Chimes. Gladiolas and bachelor's buttons planted in the garden. I am letting the weeds grow. The birdcage you gave me – we were children and I dreamed you died and were carried away by crows – has rusted open. The robins and sparrows you captured between infrequent visits do not visit anymore. I went to buy birdseed to keep them around, but the price had risen, and I didn't have a coupon.

Vacuuming and dusting. I become the local cleaning lady. Swabbing inlaid wooden decks, watering flowers never touched, never noticed. The carpet fringe will never lay flat and straight no matter how many times I bend to smooth it. If only the fringe were woven together, it would never fall out of line.

You do not come home for Christmas, and I don't spread myself in the snow. The angel you tried to freeze is decaying. Diapers and curdled breast milk.

Her first word is Da-da. An artist, perhaps.

I chase you through fog to the sound of women whispering Hail Marys over teacups.

I tear off pieces of the scones you airmail and stick them between Eleanor's wet gums. Crumbs stuck on the tiny hairs of her cheeks.

As I push her stroller through town and gossips' sneers, I pretend you amble with me. Mother says she has your eyes. I fear the day she'll see the sun and realize that as it sets here, it rises somewhere else. I nail a compass rose to the crib's headboard.

The movie theatre across from the house you grew up in is torn down today. Front-page story. Eleanor helps me drag one of the seat-rows home from the auction. I only wanted one, but they're welded together in three. Of course. Hammering it into the living-room floor.

She is learning to tap dance. Wants to be Ginger Rogers or Fred Astaire. Ribbons in her braids.

The steel mill is hiring third shift. Mother will watch Eleanor through the night.

I step on a forgotten nail on my way to the mailbox, its point sticking through the other side, an inch below my big toe. Blood and bandages. Mother says it is a sign. She does not say of what.

I find a straw pressed between the pages of my Bible. Ninth grade when you took me to The Parlor for hamburgers. You had coke, I had 7-Up. I held the bottle to my eye and you kaleidoscoped into so many eyes and mouths. Your teeth marks still on the straw. Do your other lovers notice the habit? No one uses straws these days, at least, no world traveler.

Today my horoscope says seven will be my lucky number. Seven stitches in my palm from a slip while slicing onions. Crying and bleeding – hand above heart. The blood drips into the cutting board's grain. The black thread train-tracks across my lifeline. The doctor said these stitches don't dissolve once the wound heals. I'll have to go back.

We are losing, I think.

A cardinal flew into my windshield. Feathers like shrapnel. I cannot drive again. I refuse.

The woman next door locks the windows and takes a nap in her oven. She isn't found for weeks because the smell is trapped. Eleanor and I aren't able to cook dinner.

I sculpt your eyelids and forehead. A bust. Cut a slit in the slippery clay for the change slot. I keep my pennies in your head after you are fired. Eleanor uses you as a jewelry box, hanging necklaces and ribbons over the porcelain. I set you on the kitchen counter next to the Humpty Dumpty cookie jar.

Please come home. I am trying to teach Eleanor how to make persimmon pudding – your favorite – but she hates persimmons and ovens. A good Gretel.

Eleanor and I watch the Travel Channel in hope. She likes sitting in the middle chair from the theatre.

I bought a bicycle at the pawnshop. (People do pawn suitcases.) It came with a child's seat, but Eleanor is too heavy and we can't make it up hills. We take turns running beside each other. Soon, we'll buy another. A first-aid kit in the handlebar basket to repair the animals thrown to the shoulder. There are so many undone.

Your package came today.

Eleanor and I roast hot dogs over the stove. Glad gas is included in rent.

A globe in the library. I point out the places you have been. She runs her fingers over the texture of geography, blowing off dust. To gauge the distance between where we are and you are, I touch one side while Eleanor touches the other. You are further than our hands can span.

The gifts are...

Eleanor shakes the castanets you sent every chance she can get, through breakfast and television commercials. Wants to know if there's a castanet-er position in the school band. I suggest a petition and pour more orange juice.

The concrete cracks in the porch stairs are widening. I dream of spindles and sleeping one hundred years, or as many as it takes until I can't blame you for turning at the sight of thorns. Eleanor wants bedtime stories, but all I have are postcards.

A gray hair in my cereal. At first, I didn't know whose it was.

A bonfire of your ink. I add leaves, branches, and Eleanor's 2T and 6X clothing to make it last longer. My feet pounding a rhythm you hear in the voice of a Vietnamese waiter or train-track shove. Tell me you hear me. Tell me at least once you drummed your fingers inside frustration.

Mother brings blueberry muffins and sleeping pills. Places self-help books around the house, as if those crumbs can lead to anywhere but here.

Eleanor stops dancing. Her toes and heels are softening.

Of course, you arrive in the town's only taxi. Neighbors lean over balconies to watch. I don't run into the street, arms wide.

34

I turn up the radio and light a cigarette. Wicker biting. You tip
your hat to the driver but leave it on as you cross the sidewalk.
Suitcases evolved from sticker-clad vinyl to expensive leather
with wheels. Eleanor is in bed with breasts and cramps, heating
pad pressed to belly. She can hear your voice but cannot yet
detect what it is laced with. You drop glass birds into my lap.
I turn my head from your kiss. Your smell is new this time.
The dusky scent of a middle-aged man.

She knows who you are. She whispers how handsome, a Gene
Kelly. I remind her that he's an actor. That Brigadoon appears
every three hundred years for no good reason.

I close my eyes. You roll to the other side of the bed. I want
to build another bonfire. You light the cigarette we used to
share, our fingers grazing as we passed it back and forth. How
many cigarettes have you lit while I helped Eleanor with her
lessons or laughed at her knock-knock jokes two thousand
clocks away? But tonight, you don't even ask if I care for
a drag. I want you to, so I can tell you of the day Eleanor
came home from school crying because there was a lecture
on cancer complete with slides of charred lungs, faces void
of noses, lips. Holes in throats where words fester.

Eleanor sits in the middle while you struggle with the screen
and projector. I try to smile between popcorn kernels. A twelve-
year slide show: proof of your productivity. Mine is blinding at
yours right now. At number thirty, I stop counting the recurring
smiling woman dressed like a magazine ad for beautiful. We
all reach into the popcorn bowl. Our hands touch. We pull
away and rearrange the throw pillows – decoration an easier
issue. Eleanor runs to the bathroom to floss her teeth because
of the school assembly about tooth decay. A brief glance and
your fingers are at the nape of my neck. Those amnesiac
fingers. In this second hand's tick, I want to forget the white

35

space between slides and fall into memory, immune to possible suffocation. Eleanor returns, laughing at the butter and cheese smears on our faces and chests. Use the flash.

I see the rabbit before you can brake. Eleanor screams. You whistle with the radio. The rabbit shakes, drags itself across the road. You refuse to stop. By the time we get to the shopping mall, I'm crying and Eleanor is humming like she does when she's upset – a habit she never has noticed. I could have rescued it, cradled it to me, pressed my lips to the patches of lost hair as we rushed to the vet. You are ruffled, shoving fingers through your hair as always. You stare into the rearview mirror and accuse her of taking after her mother. As if I'm not here, perhaps locked in a tall tower. I cross myself, giggling deep in relief.

After dinner, I unfold the baby bonnets, blankets, my scrap-books of Eleanor. Of you. Head in hands, you crumple in the sofa. She watches from the crack of her bedroom door. A castanet hits the wall and shatters, rice falling as if a wedding. Not ours. Never ours.

Let's fly a kite, you say. Eleanor drags behind us on the way to the park. The hill is much smaller than I remember from when we climbed up there and held hands. Eleanor lies on the hill's hip, tickling dandelions. You hold the string as I struggle to steady the paper diamond into the wind. Eleanor watches our *Mary Poppins* moment. You wrap your arms around my waist. The kite unleashes from my fingers. You say I should understand. The red diamond catches in the trees below. Branches rip the flimsy architecture. She doesn't jump or try to reach the flapping string. Once, in a crowded diner, I held a green bottle that shattered your face into so many that I couldn't find the original.

Eleanor sits beside you as you show her all the pictures you never took of us. When I was younger, Mother cleaned the house when she was angry with Father. Spring cleaning twenty times a year. I'd sit in the middle of the living room as she roared around me, dust swirling, trinkets lifted and replaced. Already, Eleanor seems to understand you better than I ever will. I walk to the Laundromat. For one spin cycle, I'm seven again sitting on the counter as Mother folds sheets and you haven't moved to the neighborhood yet and all is mountain rain detergent. On my way home, a turtle rests in the middle of the road. I drop the laundry basket and run. Its head will turn too slow to even register that it must move. Smashed shell of age by color. I hold it against my chest and carry it to the grass on the side of the road it was headed. I wait until the legs unfold, scales rippling orange. My mother and I used to race turtles in our backyards, balloons taped to shells in case we might lose track.

Promises of postcards and pictures. Eleanor says don't worry. I warn her of 7-Up bottles. She waves from the porch. I go into her room where her crib still stands under piles of folded clothes that are out of season, or outgrown.

Sanctuary

Pete steps from the truck – *Pete's Moving* on the door – and into the church parking lot.

Pete always inspects a job because, more than once, someone says twenty boxes, but when he gets there it's more like a hundred, so he has to borrow the phone or drive back to the office and call in the rest of the staff – if staff is what you call a brother-in-law and nephew.

This is the first job in a month. The last time he really made money was in the '70s when the tool-and-die factory was built on the edge of town. Now work mostly comes from kids leaving for the college forty-five minutes down I-70, but more kids graduate into the factory than college.

There are the basic jobs like today that Pete can do by his lonesome. This church sold their piano to a new church. A 1-2-3 job. Load it up, drive it across town, wheel it down the ramp and into the new sanctuary. Just like that. The kind of job that, if you're considering closing the business because you can't chew another ibuprofen for back pain, makes you rationalize the harder jobs. Like when the high school lost funding for Industrial Ed., and he lifted lathe and table saw and a dozen machines weighing as much as the truck cab – all the time praying for no one to stumble, the circular saw ready to slice through his very fleshy fingers.

As he walks toward the church's double-glass doors, the bottle of ibuprofen rattles in his breast pocket next to his Dorals. Over the phone, the church secretary said she'd leave the doors unlocked and that the sanctuary was to the right. Then she paused. You will be careful? The piano is very old. It's been here since the church was built. (Pete wanted to joke about the piano being as old as Jesus, but Reeva says his sense of humor amuses him more than anyone else.) Although everyone knows that the wealthiest people attend this church, he wanted to ask the secretary why they wouldn't *sell* an antique piano in condition good enough for playing, for shouldn't every church need money? – but a fly landed on his sandwich, so he swatted it away and forgot.

When he used to try to make Reeva talk about how she won't go to church because she can't bear to hear a baby cry or laugh during the service, all she'd say was, Prayers don't work. Reeva and he haven't attended a church since their third pregnancy. As the children ran to the altar stairs to listen to the preacher's lesson, Reeva snuck to the bathroom. While the children huddled at the preacher's feet – congregation nodding and smiling – Pete sat rigid in the pew thinking of Reeva weeping in the locked stall, her hand on the flesh covering her empty uterus.

The only light in the sanctuary comes from the stained glass that provides no window onto the world. He doesn't need clear glass, though, to imagine Central Street where cars pass occasionally on their way from the cluster of fast-food restaurants near the interstate to the town center of buildings that once held businesses instead of For Rent signs, or worse, that no longer bother holding For Rent signs. And out beyond and all around the town all the corn and bean fields, like a green or brown galaxy – depending on the season – that this very small town whirls inside, though the whirling is only obvious to those old enough to remember.

As Pete makes his way down the aisle, his question about why the church isn't selling the piano is answered by a sleek baby grand. This church will never beg for alms.

He has to squeeze between the glistening orchestral piece and altar to get to the back wall where the ancient upright stands.

Pete leans against the upright to check its weight. The secretary guessed it weighed seventy pounds; Pete smiled into the phone at that one. Women think only humans weigh over a hundred pounds, and everything else weighs either less than or as much as a truck. If they just remembered one bag of potting soil is forty pounds, things would run smoother.

He can't fit a four-wheeler in the space between the wall and piano. If access to the back of this piano is necessary for tuning, nobody has tuned it in a long time. He touches a key. A long, long time.

He moves the piano bench to the side then grips beneath the keyboard and pulls. Wood creaks. The bones inside his knees creak. He adjusts his weight, pulls more. The piano bumps a foot across the carpet.

After the second miscarriage, Reeva's counselor suggested a hobby. Because Reeva always wanted piano lessons as a girl, Pete called up a rental center in the next town over and had a piano delivered. A year later the repo man rang the doorbell. For a second, Pete sees Reeva standing between their piano and the repo man, her arms extended and shaking, begging him not to take the piano from her. But you didn't pay, the man said. Reeva misheard him and began screaming, *I did pray, I did pray, I did!*

A thin veneer covers the back of the old piano and is peeling. Probably won't survive the move. Pete'll have to fix it. He nods and returns to the truck for his toolbox. Not for the first time does he pat his shoulder for carrying a toolbox. More than once during a job, he has bumped a chair arm or table out of whack. Usually, a few nails or hammers are enough. On rare occasions, he takes the item to his office, sands it down, re-stains or paints it, then returns it with an apology for accidentally leaving this in the truck, hope you haven't worried – thus saving money and possibly a trip to the local law office.

Pete rummages in the truck for the toolbox and blankets to protect the piano. The urge to smoke creeps up his throat. He swallows. He'll wait until the piano is loaded. He's quitting again. Rather, Reeva decided. Usually, she gets on her soapbox after a trip to the doctor, all that time sitting in the waiting room reading pamphlet reasons for death.

This time she woke him up in the middle of the night. She was standing above him. He didn't hear her until she said pregnant. She said, You quit smoking every time. But you never had a reason not to start again. If you had held just one baby, you would have quit, which means I'm why you're killing yourself. I'm sorry, she said. Then she slid open the glass door and walked into the backyard out to the row of lilies.

Lifting the piano slightly off the floor as he pulls it from the wall, he sticks his arm between the wall and piano, pulling. The keys rise and fall, a hum crescendoing through the sanctuary. He startles at the sound and lowers the upright. He forgot to move the baby grand out of the way. He takes off his baseball hat and rubs his forehead. This is supposed to be an easy job. Look at yourself. A cigarette will clear your head.

Pete puts his hat back on and focuses his weight on his legs like Reeva reminds him when he's pleading a bad back as why he wants to sleep. The truth is he doesn't want a bedtime embrace to turn into anything more. But he's learned when truth in marriage leads to disaster – when truth should simply become a secret. Long ago were the nights when their embrace held no ghosts within it.

Of course the baby grand slides easily, wheels slick with factory oil.

He picks up the sheet music lamp and sets it on the upright so he can see to fix the peeling veneer. It's the same dark wood as the rest of the piano. No particleboard or plywood in those days. A handle once attached to the bottom, but it isn't there now. Only the wounds left from the nails. Nails have been planted around the veneer's perimeter. As he raises the veneer, the nails fall out and lose themselves in the plush red carpet. The cover comes off in his hands.

A large doll is his first thought.

He steps back.

He turns to see if anyone else sees the doll stuck in the back of the piano, a doll the size of a seven-year-old girl.

But it isn't a doll.

A little girl.

Or what is left.

A corpse stuck in the piano this church hired Pete to load, drive across town, and load into another church.

But is it a corpse if there is no flesh?

Her dress is old, white and faded like her bones. Victorian. The lace at her wrists like the intricate droplets Reeva tatted for the bassinet coverlet before and during the first pregnancy. And after the miscarriage – that forsaken year between the first miscarriage and the next time she smiled a real smile – she filled her lap with lace then pulled it apart then tatted it again.

Battenburg lace.

Pete remembers because when he asked her what it was called – trying to get her to talk about anything – he thought she had called it Batman's lace.

Battenburg lace in Reeva's lap and now on the corpse's dress, though, of course, the lace on the dress has been here all along.

Even though the girl's bones show through the fabric, he still thinks porcelain doll. Her bisque face turned from whoever put her in here. Her ear vibrating as the piano hammers struck the strings all these years. She's from the world of tea parties on tiny round tables in backyards shadowed by four-storey houses. But her body is like one of the mannequins in the thrift store display window. Discolored by sun, missing fingers.

Pete turns his head away, but it's too late. The little girl in the piano will play his nightmares the rest of his life. As his eyes close, she'll pop in and wave her fingers to bone. In some, she will be a doll Pete gives to Reeva. Reeva runs to play with her in the very empty nursery, and Pete chases after Reeva, trying to warn her that the doll is not a child, but when he finally catches up, the girl is cradling Reeva whose thighs are covered in blood and tissue. The girl turns and her jaw clanks. Papa, I don't want to practice my scales anymore. Or she's in the entertainment center, the refrigerator, his grandmother's casket. Peek-a-boo, Papa! You found me fast this time.

Pete can easily slip one arm beneath the doll's or girl's or corpse's or bones' knees and pick her up like he carried Reeva to bed when they were first married and his back was good and he still imagined carrying their future children like his dad carried him from the car to the house after a long day at the ballpark.

But this girl has no bedroom. Her parents are dead and the tree swing she spun circles in has collapsed or been bulldozed under the house, under weeds. So many abandoned houses tilt along the country roads. Which one is it?

He should cross the parking lot to the gas station and call the police and wait until Harry drives in, tips his sheriff hat, and says, what seems to be the trouble? And Pete will lead him to the piano.

Maybe Harry will string yellow caution tape around the church or just between the pews and altar. Everyone in town will learn soon enough of the breaking story and ring the parsonage phone until the preacher's wife finally answers and says, yes, there will still be church, and no, no one knows who she is, but the funeral is in three days.

The whole town will attend. Everyone wants to peer into the eye sockets that have watched the church for ninety years. After the service – maybe at this church instead of the funeral home – everyone will pile into their cars and drive slowly down Central where, on weekends, teenagers cruise, honking at each other and parking at the gas station up by the interstate or down by the grain elevators until someone of age buys wine coolers and then they head out to a cemetery to fondle or tip tombstones.

The funeral goers crowd in the cemetery under the bright

43

blue tent. Pete and staff carry the casket to its metal stand. The preacher says another prayer. The children's choir sings this little light of mine. Everyone who hasn't wept does now. Women press bosoms. Men bow heads or hold wives or palm their children's heads. That night and every night until their own deaths, the fondling teenagers will avoid the girl's head-stone, but their grandchildren won't.

But Pete can't cross the parking lot yet because something's rubbing him wrong. The little girl does need to rest in peace. That's not the trouble. When he was a boy, he walked to the diner every day in case the next *Batman* comic was in. He'd sit at the counter, sipping a cherry coke until the doorknob bells jangled and in came the comic-book deliveryman. The owner would then cut the cord and hand him the top issue. There on the barstool little Pete would sit, admiring the cleanness, the oil-slick cover as if Batman hand-painted it for him. His. All his.

When Reeva had a yard sale to raise money to begin the adoption process and he saw her carrying his comics down from the attic, he took the box from her arms. He tried to explain that these comics weren't for just any stranger. *Anyone* would not have the right reverence for the superhero unlike other superheroes. Batman didn't have special powers. A man with intelligence and money, he became the man that any boy, but especially Petie, could be. And now, could have been.

And this girl, what? This girl is what could happen to any girl. Or boy. What if this was his little girl, a fifth pregnancy that lived through every trimester and all the way to her seventh birthday? Pete rocks at the thought.

Sleeping Beauty.

But she's not waking up, Petie. Nobody can change that. Not you. Not Batman. Not God. Maybe it could've changed back when, but Pete is not of the camp who believes comfort comes from saying Everything Happens For A Reason.

At the very least, someone could have found her so her

parents could stop hoping. Pete knows what hope does to a person. Reeva hunched at the piano saying, Wanna hear a song I wrote today? Reeva smashing her arms and chest across the piano keys. I've named it *Miscarriage No. 4.*

Surely, church members and the town searched for the girl. While men and women walked through cornfields calling the girl's name and watching the ground at their feet, the pianist played every Sunday, through everyone praying for the girl's safe return. Jesus.

And the smell. Not for one day but weeks. Maybe the girl died around Christmas when the sanctuary is decked with greenery and the Christmas tree stands next to the pulpit and piano. The elderly pianist could have lost her sense of smell – that happens – and if there were complaints, the preacher answered by cleaning the mousetraps. Maybe the soil in the folds of her dress means someone buried her then dug her up, stuffing her in here because the police sniffed too close. Or maybe she was nailed in at – according to the tiny gold tag on the lip of the keyboard – the Oregon, Illinois piano factory in 1908. Pete wishes the tag wasn't there. Or at least that he didn't read it. Pete thinks of her tombstone. Engraved time.

What if the town named her after the piano? Little girl Schiller. Pete shudders. Oregon Schiller on her gravestone. That's what they'll write in her obituary, thinking they're clever, as if finding her brings her to life, ready to be named. After the first miscarriage, Reeva said they shouldn't pick a name until the doctor handed them the very alive baby.

Pete digs the rag out of his back pocket and wipes his face.

Be a doll, he says. Dissonant with hope, his voice surrounds him, shocking him to his knees. The piano cover falls to the side.

A cigarette. Need a cigarette. No. Haven't done anything yet. Hey, buddy, you just opened a cold file like on that TV show Reeva watches. Every case is just like this, Petie. Set in a small town where real crime never happens so when it does, no one's caught. One year. Two years. Twenty years. The police no longer get phone calls from the mother who hopes her daughter isn't buried twenty miles away or a husband asking where the bastard is who cut his wife into a jigsaw puzzle and sealed the pieces in a fifty-gallon drum. And here you are, Petie, the rookie who picks up an old file as the local newspaper gets a letter full of tips and CON BRIO! the case is opened and solved in forty minutes of TV time.

He picks up the veneer and leans it against the communion railing. He moves the piano bench beside her and sits down. Sure, the other church expects him to arrive about now and Reeva's setting the oven timer on dinner, but this girl had time. Time that should've – or, at least, could've – been spent elsewhere. She could have been one of his grandmother's play-mates. His grandmother never mentioned any missing girl, but eventually, missing girls turn into folklore and find themselves in the hands of children clapping and singing during recess. *Little Bonnie Knell/ Fell into a Well/ Until the Drought the Water/ Covered up the Smell.*

Even if the smell left in the winter, the flies would have known. One common housefly riding in on a lady's hat could fly into the space cut for the piano pedals and settle for life on the girl, create a whole family – generations of families in a few sermons. The congregation couldn't have missed so many flies. They would have thought of the plagues. They would have taken the flies as a sign. They love signs. So, what if the church knew and didn't want anyone to know? *You will be careful – the piano is very old.* After all, he and Reeva didn't tell anyone about her miscarriages after the first one. *Guess what I've named it? Miscarriage No. 4!*

Pete pats down his pocket and lifts out his cigarettes without thinking. The cellophane wrapper crinkles in the sanctuary like when he was a boy and during sermons his grandmother unwrapped lemon drops so slowly that his ears burned. Pete returns the cigarettes to his pocket and chews an ibuprofen instead. The taste is bitter, feels right.

No longer white, her stockings lead into black shoes that button up the sides. Shoes that require a hook for fastening. Wealthy. A child of an oil man, perhaps. One of the many who capitalized on the oil that swelled the town's population at the century's turn, then left when the oil did.

He can take her home to Reeva. They can bury her in the backyard along the row of lilies, hold a little service like they have for each miscarriage. Reeva got the idea when a car hit the neighbor's cat, and the neighbor boy watched his father roll it into the ditch. The next day the boy stood at the ditch with a shovel, his head bowed. Pete argued against the idea at first – Too morbid, he said. It's not morbid, it's our child, she said.

He built a casket for the porcelain doll Reeva bought. They had nothing else to bury. He said a few words then she kneeled, patting and smoothing the dirt. Too many years found them standing over a new casket.

You know, Pete says to the girl – no longer afraid she'll turn and look at him with ice-blue eyes – if I found you here in another hundred years, you'd probably end up in a museum. In a children's museum. Like this one Reeva and I saw on our honeymoon in San Antonio. Most of the museum was taxidermied animals in plastic habitats. Each habitat had a button, and when you pressed the button, a light shined on the animal and a recorded man's voice narrated each animal's story, but none of the animals had a unique story. Each story was merely about all finches like this stuffed finch, all jackrabbits like this dead jackrabbit.

Pete closes his mouth.

The animals were falling apart. Seams pulling, fur patchy.

The recorded man knew nothing about what this specific butterfly saw as it migrated from the Midwest to Mexico, how

47

the wind felt against its silk wings. The veins in its wings like Battenburg lace.

He imagines the girl in a glass room next to the last bear shot out of Eastern Texas. She's posed on a piano bench, her back to the kiddies pawing the glass, her fingers sealed to the piano keys. Someone pushes the button. The light shines down and a recorded choir sings Jesus loves me, this I know or hide it under a bushel – no! – I'm gonna let it shine.

The keys move up and down.

Her body jerks along with the music.

The kiddies roll their eyes and say bo-ring and pull their mothers away. Maybe one child stops and wonders what the little girl had nightmares about, or if she hula-hooped, or if she even played piano or if some curator merely decided that she did.

Pete snaps open his toolbox and pulls out the finishing nails. If the girl were ever afraid of the dark, she's forgotten by now. He fits the veneer back on. He waits for his hands to steady before hammering the first nail. He sees her sitting outside in the grass behind the church, reading her bible and waiting for her brother to bicycle up and walk her home. A man in a black suit and derby strolls up behind her, and as she sees his shadow fall in front of her, his hands wrap her throat.

Pete pulls another nail.

A group of children run into the sanctuary and hide under pews, felt banners, in the choir loft. One little girl lifts up the piano cover and climbs inside. A little boy shouts ready or not and skips in. She doesn't know she's been found because her back's to him. The little boy pushes the piano, wheels oil-slick from the factory, against the wall. Clever boy who knows the piano is for lessons and the organ for services, so it won't matter if the sound is slightly muffled. And then the church is closed all week and by Sunday, she's too faint to scream. By the next, she's dead and swelling.

48

Pete cries and hammers another nail.

Three little girls say let's play Jesus. One climbs into the piano, which is now the cave, and the girls roll her against the wall, and inside, the girl waits to be resurrected, but the girls leave and run barefoot outside, laughing because that'll teach her to put on airs about her fancy shoes. They plan to return in three days...

Pete throws the blanket over the piano. He wraps duct tape around and around. He places the piano bench upside down on the lid. Up the aisle, outside. Up the ramp. He belts it at the very front, by the window that looks into the cab. He drives across town to the new church that maybe Reeva and he will attend on Sunday. His arm dangles out the window, his fingers hammering the door.

Raw as Hands

My twin sister washes her hands until they bleed. The bathroom mirror reflects her parted hair, furrowed brow. After she towels her hands dry, she hovers over the doorknob and can't remember washing her hands. Unsure and unable to convince herself otherwise, she bends again to the faucet. Rewind. Play. Rewind. Play. Tears splashing off her burning knuckles, chapped joints. Rewind. Play.

When we were little, before she washed her hands and cried into towels, she screamed. At the dinner table, after communion, in the park – the park seems like a place where children can use their outside voices, yelling with pleasure at the rush of a swing or slide. Her scream was not like this. Sometimes, soprano-scraping, other times, gasping-frantic. One time, the one I remember most (like the time I fell out of a swing and lost five teeth, mouthful of blood and bone), she opened her mouth – we were all ready to embrace her, sing nursery rhymes, leave the room – and I didn't hear that scream again until years later when a bat hung from my bathroom ceiling. When I finally got it down, I trapped a bowl over it. As I slid a paper plate under the bowl, ready to toss it out the window, I accidentally squeezed a wing. The bat panicked and out came my sister's sound.

There are others like her, but they come in various forms. I began researching them, needing to prove to our parents it wasn't their fault or mine.

Some won't leave their homes because they fear murdering someone. They won't, of course. But that's what they think.

Some find themselves crouched over rugs at 3 AM, straightening carpet fringe. Others worry about hurting their unborn or unconceived children.

But those are different matters, other sisters' stories.

My twin sister washes her hair, sudsing, rinsing, and

resoaping. She steps from the shower and turban-towels her head. Shaves her legs from the bathtub's edge. When she gets to the door, she stops. Then she gets back in the shower.

My sister has seen counselors since kindergarten. They say, Imagine not washing your hands. They say, Imagine yourself swimming in an ocean of pencils. I used to tell her to give them chances. I used to believe the counselors over her. Maybe I was like the people who believe in God and coincidences.

When she's busy, she's fine. But in those silences, those what-shall-I-do-now moments, it's hard. Like when Grandmother died. Grandfather held his tears through the funeral, through packing off gardening gloves and costume jewelry (saving her housecoat with the cigarette burns) until he found himself in the living room, staring at the steamer trunk she brought from the old country as a child – it was then he cried.

When we go to restaurants, my sister locates the bathroom like people check for orange EXIT signs.

There are so many faucets.

My friends were scared of her and their mothers wouldn't let them come over to play. In high school we made fun of her. I shouldn't have. Her hand washing was beginning, but I didn't know how bad it was. I thought she was vain. She's never been beautiful by most people's standards. She has this hollow-haunted look. It's not in her eyes but in how she moves. I have to watch her touch me to be sure she did. If I don't, I have to rewind to remember if we did hug. If I forget to keep my eyes open, it feels like we're merging. As if when I look in the mirror, my reflection will be hers.

When we go shopping, she never touches anything. Maybe it's just me, but I like to touch racks of satin dresses or slide a finger along the grain of a chair. I hand-weigh fruit from grocery-store bins. She doesn't. If she does buy something, she waits I'm ready to leave before she picks up the item. If there's a line, I go outside to smoke while she roams the store.

We called her names. Ghost, Invisible, Band-Aid – she wore

Band-Aids like bracelets. They tripped her in gym class. They butted in front of her in the cafeteria. One time in algebra – it was almost Halloween – the cheerleaders who sat behind me were planning their costumes. One let out a scream then whispered, I'll go as Invisible. The whole class pounded their desks, choked on giggles. My sister sat in the back row. I secretly hoped she saw my shaking shoulders, thrown-back laugh. It felt almost orgasmic (as I would find out the next summer in my boyfriend's swimming pool) to let her know I didn't care anymore. That I'm not her.

We look more alike now. Back then, I tried my damnedest to avoid association. Crimping my dyed hair, caking eyeliner, saving allowance for months to buy name-brand jeans and sweaters. I talked loud, clipping syllables like coupons. We were never the twins who got kicks out of switching places. Everyone else kept us separate, too. Relatives went out of their way to talk to her. She didn't help, always nailing herself to the walls – eyes closed – eventually disappearing to an empty room.

She stayed home for college. I moved. A comfort at first, Mother's letters assured me that my old world still existed. Your sister loves her classes, especially calculus. She's at a movie right now with Will, whom I think she might be dating (!). She misses you, sleeps in your bed. Asks if you called. A lot of showers. The bathroom never seems vacant. The water bill. Three laundry loads of towels. A new counselor. I wish I didn't have to worry. She was such a happy baby. Ticklish, chatty. Such a pleasure (you both were, of course). I really wish you could find the time to call her or send a card. You can't be *that* busy. Do you remember when –

I stopped opening the letters.

We had the same nightmares. When I realized no one liked her (even me), I moved to a different room. Even if she did have my thoughts, I pretended she didn't. It was scary how easy it was to turn away. When we awoke from the same nightmare, I waited, listening to her rise from her bed and cross the hallway to my room, ready to whisper and hold hands like we once did to forget. She'd stand there at my pillow, streetlight shining through her nightgown, as I lied and said I didn't dream of the woman who recited lullabies while pushing her baby's face into water.

Before breaking pencils or washing her hands, it was numbers. When we were on the drive toward a family vacation, I pointed out how I liked to see where cars were from. After about an hour of peering out the windshield, she began slamming her head against the seat because her brain wouldn't stop. License plate numbers poured out of her eyes and ears. Dad pulled over and carried her to the shoulder. Held her on his lap, stroking her hair and covering her eyes with his very strong hands until her body stopped panting.

She visited me at college once. The first time I'd seen her in two years.

I met her at the train station and watched me jump off the train. Red sweater, jean skirt, combat boots. I grimaced. As always, I tried to convince myself that lots of people wore this combination, that our wearing the same outfit was mere coincidence. Perhaps she saw the same chain department-store mannequin wearing this outfit, so naturally, we both put it together.

Nonetheless, when she opened her arms, I fell into them, suddenly aware of how tired I was. My chin nestled in her collarbone. She leaned her head against mine. At least, I think she did. Her first word, Bathroom?

She told obscene jokes, chain-smoked clove cigarettes (we shared the addiction). I dismissed the concern in my mother's letters – the forever-foggy bathroom mirror – as paranoia. But when we went to dinner, she stayed in the bathroom for ten minutes the first time. A line began outside the women's sign. Two trips between cigarettes and two bottles of merlot. Five minutes after the plates were cleared. Her hands were dry and cracking. When she opened her mouth, I was sure she'd scream.

You're wondering why I'm here, she said. Maybe afraid that I have something important to tell you, or maybe to propose a duel for past wrongs.

I imagined a ghost town. Our shadows striding in opposite directions. Would I turn and crouch, then shoot? Or would I shoot while throwing my body out of the way?

You think I'm trying to be a martyr, she said. For attention. You think I'm selfish, needlessly torturing Mom and Dad. I think the same things. Not that I have to explain. You probably read about it in some psychology 101 class.

What if I jumped and she crouched?

She rubbed out the cigarette, blinked 1234. It's my brain, she said. It won't cooperate. I just can't be convinced. Blood makes me sick. Any sign of contamination. I'm working on that in counseling right now. That it's my brain's fault, not mine. It's silly –

No, it's not.

She smiled.

Vampires have no reflection, I thought.

You're right, she said, they don't.

She laughed, lowering her chin but raising her pupils. The dim lighting made her. She smirked my smirk. Even at opposite ends of the ghost town, our expressions were the same.

But I'm no more one than you. She handed me a cigarette. Your mind is stronger than mine, though. Maybe I envy you. She reached over and snapped a match for me. I see blood and have to shower, wash my hands. I think disease, contamination, disease.

Don't tell me these –

I can admit I have a problem. Her voice raised, her knuckles seemingly made of the glass that held the wine she clutched. But *you*, she said. Pasting on fake nails to avoid biting yours until they bleed –

Her words fell across my thoughts a tenth of a second before she said them.

You touch yourself to fall asleep –

Please –

Even though you're more awake after orgasm after boring orgasm.

The waiter turned on his heel with the coffeepot.

I'd shoot first. It wouldn't even matter how I turned. I'd shoot first and watch her fall.

You don't make love, she said. You fasten yourself to the bedposts until you can't feel.

The couple at the booth behind us pressed their heads together.

Until, she said, you're as raw as my hands.

She closed her eyes.

I saw that I held my arm where, beneath the sweater, a yellow-purple ring rippled where my boyfriend bit me – like a minnow biting at the surface of a pond. This one wasn't as bad as some. Sometimes, it hurt to wear heavy fabric, lift a carton of milk. Sometimes, I thought his mind had split and he'd kill me. And then I started to need it, to be punished for my nightmares and thoughts. One night, as he clamped my wrists to the floral sheets, I realized why my sister washes her hands.

I'd shoot twice. Head and heart.

We pushed the restaurant's doors into the jazz. We walked in the direction of my apartment. It was cold, the last crisp shudder of autumn. Leaves shattering under our feet. We didn't wait for cars or green lights. I didn't try to escape the rhythm of our steps. I like to think we were alone in our own thoughts at that point. I was lifting her pale body from the dust, wiping the blood from her mouth. Her eyes glazed, her hands palm-up on the ground.

Every Good Girl Does Fine

This is the last practice for the year. Choir Director says, All your mothers brought treats for snack time. Our final performance is Sunday, so we must let our voices be the very best. After practice, we'll have treats in the church basement.

I want to ask her what kinds of treats, but she starts swinging her arms. The organist begins playing. The organist's hair is white like our robes. White as the divinity my mother whips up when she's up to here with the holidays.

Jimmy breaks in on the wrong measure.

Susan's off-key.

Choir Director mouths the words for the kids who can't read music and squirm the most. Spit collects in the corners of her mouth.

Choir Director never asks what we want to sing. She thinks her songs are the best, which is prideful and so God better be paying attention. At least we can wear our robes today. They are satiny smooth. Everyone in church says we're God's little angels. This is a bit wrong because girls can't be angels, but I don't say anything because it's not nice to tell adults they're ignorant, even if they are.

Sometimes, after practices, I sit on Organist's lap and pretend my feet are hers as they prance the pedals. When I'm tall enough, I'll take lessons. I'll make the pipes flap open and the whole congregation will wish there wasn't a sermon and that I'd play all morning. I'll jazz it up. They'll clap and yell amen and stand even if they're not able like in my friend's church. The only downside about her church is that the devil is always tricking them, and if they stay tricked then they'll burn in a thousand fires for longer than humans live. Luckily, I'm Methodist, so all we worry about is how much money goes into the offering plate so we can pay off the extra parking lot.

But I can't sit on Organist's lap today because I'm gonna be first to the snacks. I have to get there before Choir Director so when she metronome-taps my shoulder and says, No seconds, I will say, I haven't had any yet, Miss Director. And she will say, God does not like greedy children. And I will say, God does not like the songs you choose.

After the one billionth time singing the song, Choir Director finally says practice is over. I crouch, ready to run to the basement, hang up my robe, and eat my firsts. But now she's reminding us to line up in the choir room on Sunday after eating the glazed doughnuts and red Kool-Aid that are always in the kitchen after Sunday school. We don't have memories like our grandparents, so why's she wasting our time?

Be careful, she says, of your angel voices. Please refrain from yelling and shouting at your school picnics.

That reminds me that summer is almost here which means swimming at the park pool every day and eating peppermint patties at the concession stand and this year I'll jump off the high dive instead of crying like a ninny and being led back down the ladder by the lifeguard.

She says, Walk like ladies and gentlemen to the basement.

Dad is always telling me to act like a lady, and I am sick of it. I'd like to know who this lady is I'm impersonating because I want to kick dirt on her dress.

Organist plays the Charlie Brown song. We laugh because church isn't the place for cartoons. I've got my robe over my head before we reach the bottom of the stairs. My head gets stuck in the neck hole. Someone pushes me.

When I get into the robe room, everybody's already there. We pull and yell and grab the hangers with our names on them. Organist is still playing upstairs. The fan that makes the organ make sound is whirling fast.

I say, I'm gonna get firsts!

Jimmy calls me Mary Magdalene.

I call him Heathen, which is what Mom calls Dad when he won't hurry up on Sundays.

Jimmy head butts me in the chest. I fall into Susan. Susan falls backwards. I grab at her robe, but the satin slips through my fingers. The corner of Susan's robe catches in the organ's fan's blades. Her mouth opens like an organ pipe, but no sound comes out. Jimmy double-times it up the stairs to tell Organist to stop playing. The fan spins Susan closer. She reaches out for us. The belt slaps her thighs. Over and over. Her white tights burn black. They tear. There's a smell like when Mom lit her cigarette too close to the stove and lost her right eyebrow.

We yell, Susan!

We yell, Fire!

Preacher runs in. Preacher plays tug of war with Susan and the fan belt. Her robe isn't white anymore. She cries off-key. Preacher holds her in his arms. I pat her hand. I say, Your legs look like jellyrolls. Then I push through the children and run to the snack table.

The Only Child

Father takes us to work because babysitter can't play with us anymore. She never liked our games. He says, Don't disturb me and when I'm done we'll have ice cream.

Will we each get a cone?

He says, We'll share. We must learn how to share. Now go play in the break room until I come find you.

We say, Hide and seek?

He doesn't answer. He's not very good at that game, but he is better than babysitter. We had to show her where to hide, but her arm dangled out.

There is cherry Kool-Aid in the break room. We ask whose it is. No one appears to claim it. We can't read yet so no one's name is on the pitcher. When we drink it, our heads hit the ceiling. When we drink the rest, we fall to the ground and are as small as guinea pigs so we can't reach the pitcher on the table. We leave the break room. It is nice not to have a babysitter who says sugar eats your tongue out.

We find stairs and run up and down them. Our apartment doesn't have stairs. Cement blocks with boards don't count.

When we are out of breath and holding our sides, we slide down the railing. There's a door. It is black and has a word. We say, Where's this door lead? We say, Let's find out.

But we can't reach the doorknob so we stick our fingers to the back of our mouths where the jiggly thing hangs. Then we go back to normal size. The doorknob won't budge. It takes all our hands to turn it. We make a creaking sound as it opens.

The room is bigger than our apartment. It's as big as babysitter's church. We weren't allowed to run and yell in there.

Father would love this place because there are filing cabinets on every wall. When Father gets the raise that's coming to

him, we'll move into a house with room for his filing cabinets.
Then he won't have to keep his filing cabinets in the bedroom.
Father says it's no fun to mix work and play. Maybe that's
why babysitter didn't want to hide in Father's bed.

After babysitter got us in trouble, Father put locks on all
the filing cabinets so we can't climb in and scare him when
he finds us. That's too bad because his face makes us laugh
when we raise up and say hello. If his drawers were as big as
these, he wouldn't need milk crates for extra papers. But he
would not appreciate that these don't have locks. We are not
allowed in his anymore.

We ask if Father will be mad if we open one. We say, We
are earning his trust. He will trust us if we pull the handle at
the same time because then we are sharing and that would
make him happy. He needs happy more than trust. The drawer
slides nicely. We don't have to tug at all.

Inside is a person. She has red hair and no clothes. She's
alone.

We say, You must be lonely. We know how that is.

We shiver.

It is very cold in here not to have a blanket. We open and
shut other drawers but there are only people. Maybe these
cabinets have heaters since they don't hold papers or folders.
Maybe everyone is hibernating like babysitter in her no-yell
church. But babysitter wore clothes.

We go back to our redhead.

We shut her drawer.

We open it.

We say, Peek-a-boo.

We laugh.

She doesn't.

We say, You are like babysitter. Not a child or adult. And
you don't laugh at our games.

We say, What's your name? Is it Eileen like babysitter?

We say, Cat got your tongue?

We open her mouth and look. There is cottony stuff in there like dentist puts in our mouths when we've eaten too much sugar. Her tongue is the wrong color. Too bad we drank all the Kool-Aid or we could have shared. Then we see the stars in her chest.

We say, The Kool-Aid would squirt out anyway. That is a funny picture in our head so we laugh.

We touch the stars. Her belly. Her rib. Her breast.

We say, You look like babysitter, but her stars were red.

Her skin is soft like Grandmother's. Grandmother lives in New York and visited when babysitter began hibernating.

We ask the lady-girl where she's from.

We say, New York. How's the weather? Cloudy. That must be why you don't smile.

We say, How'd you get those stars?

We say, Don't play with guns or you'll learn a bad lesson. Eileen, look at our gun.

Our finger points at her breast her rib her belly.

Boom boom boom.

We cover our ears then climb into the filing cabinet.

Who turned out the lights, Eileen?

We laugh.

It's awfully cold in here. Will Father find us? He's no good at this game. I say, This time he'll look for us. This time, he'll say Gottchya! Not, What happened?

Halfway There

Natalie Schroeder's windows are rolled up. Summer won't really hit until the corn's knee-high by the fourth of July. The radio rattles the rearview mirror. Natalie drums the steering wheel to stay awake. She's just got off at the factory and has a three or four hour drive ahead of her, depending on her Yugo. She's on her way to Camp Zoom, the film camp Millie won an all-paid scholarship to attend. It's the first time Millie has been away from home. But Natalie doesn't need to worry. Millie's okay. So young. Twelve years old. Millie's fine.

Nat was napping between the factory and janitorial work when the scholarship phone call came, followed by Millie jumping on Nat's bed, sputtering Mom – phone – camp – won and lots of uhs, ahs, and I means. Nat rubbed her eyes and smiled. You got the golden ticket, huh? And with that Millie leapt out of the trailer and over the moon, singing all the way around it.

Millie's fine because of the envelope in the empty ashtray. The only letter from Millie the whole week. Millie's bubbly cursive saying what a good time she's having and I'm learning tons of stuff but it's lights out soon so I gotta go. P.S. Don't worry, Mom, and don't come early or you'll just sit in the car and wait. I'm right as rain. Love, M. Right as rain was the answer to how are you? in their trailer. Millie, I think you have a temperature – Right as rain, Mom. You look tired, Mom – Right as rain, Mill. The book Natalie plans to read is in the passenger seat.

After checking out the car yesterday, her brother said to drive it to a used car lot. Natalie laughed in his face. She saves her tears for the road home from assembling light fixtures or mopping the high school. She doesn't want to be the mother crying behind doors while the daughter tries not to listen.

What, dear brother, do you suggest I trade it for? A Cadillac? C'mon, Nat.

She shook her head.

Maybe Mom and Dad –

Natalie ruffled the hair on his eighteen-year-old head that refused to believe their good ol' Mom and Pop could stay silent on Natalie's side of the phone forever. They'd proven resilient for the nine months and twelve years since they tried to persuade her to give Millie away. Natalie gave them her love and her copy of the house key. Packed her suitcase.

Last week, Millie lugged the same suitcase up the stairs to the balcony room at camp while Natalie stood next to another mother dropping off her daughter. The woman asked Natalie why the camp wasn't at the university, as she herself took a film class there years back so they certainly have all the equipment plus the girls could stay in dorms instead of this motel in the middle of nowhere. The woman sighed before Natalie could point out that the motel wasn't nowhere; it did have a Bloomington address. The woman squinted at the sun. My little girl, she said, got the scholarship, so who am I to complain? Before Natalie could say that Millie was the one with the scholarship, the director, in a Camp Zoom T-shirt that matched all the girls' T-shirts, called the parents and campers to the center of the parking lot.

It's been right as rain so far. Just a few more hours and she and Millie will stop at the diner Millie pointed out on the drive up. A diner with a flat roof and wraparound windows. I bet it's got black and white floors, Millie yelled, wind shuffling her black curls over her face. And waitresses in poodle skirts? Nat added. Millie's eyes said WOW! in the side mirror. The menu will probably be outrageous, but if Nat gets only water and fries, it's doable. Besides, Millie deserves a treat for writing the scholarship-winning essay.

The camp director led the parents with separation anxiety on a tour of the old motel. It still had the old bulb sign out

front. The bulbs were replaced to say Camp Zoom. The
director flipped a switch, and the NO in front of VACANCY
appeared. The girls cheered. The tour didn't include the rooms
because a motel room is a motel room, right, folks? We don't
have a housekeeper, though, so the girls will have to clean up
their rooms. Good luck, a father said, and everyone laughed
and hugged and drove away, daughters waving in rearview
mirrors.

A black SUV turns onto the road from a driveway leading
to a white farmhouse and red barn and the usual clutter of silos
and tractors. She figures it won't take any time to disappear
ahead of her. The Yugo can't go above sixty anymore. The
SUV most certainly can. In the off chance it does turn left at
the junction and all the way to I-57, she'll have no way of
knowing.

But the Yugo does catch up. Through the back windshield,
Nat sees the TV screen hanging like a visor in their back seat
for the kiddies. Those poor, poor farmers, she mutters. Just
a week before, Nat drove behind a SUV that had a TV and
said what's wrong with looking out the windows? Imagination
not expensive enough? Millie nodded but kept her eyes on
the cartoon playing on the screen. They probably come with
DVDs and screens now. Like a radio or antilock brakes.
There were days, she heard her father say, when seatbelts
were optional. Optional. Well, Daddy, Nat says to the SUV,
microwaves used to be optional, but then the stove broke last
month, so it's all your granddaughter and I have.

It's dark enough for Nat to see the screen. It isn't a cartoon.
Real people. Black and white film. Millie's favorite. Rent
a horror flick in black and white and Millie forgets about
nightmares until it's over and she's sure somebody's at every
window.

The only part of camp Millie worried over was the five-
minute film each camper would make. Nat asked if she was
worried about getting an idea. Mo*ther*. It's not that; what if

they only have color film? Nat shrugged. It's free, baby. You have the rest of your life to make black and whites. Millie rolled her eyes, a recent habit. Nat stood and said, Now announcing the Academy Award for best director. And the winner is – Natalie opened her purse and pulled out her wallet – Millie Schroeder! Nat dropped her voice to a whisper, Get out of your seat and get on stage. Everyone in TV land is watching.

Millie held tight to the chair arms and bit her lip.

What's the matter? Nat asked. You don't want the award? Or are you overseas and unable to make it?

Mother, I'm not going to be a director. Or an actress. I'll be behind the camera.

Never say never, Mill.

Never, Mom.

A little girl is on the SUV screen. A little girl with black curly hair. She smiles like someone told her to. Like in the home movies Nat's dad made when she was little. Smile, Nat, show your pearly whites. But this camera doesn't shake. It zooms in on the girl's face.

A beauty mark over her left eyebrow.

Nat grips the steering wheel. She blinks. The beauty mark is still there when she opens her eyes. The beauty mark Natalie kisses before Millie falls asleep or wakes up. Right as rain, Mom. No worries.

The girl's eyes have a look Nat has seen only in nightmares. Millie falling out of a tree. Millie hitting her head on a diving board. Millie in a bathtub saying, Wynken, Blynken, and Nod one night.

The girl. It's Millie. Christ. Millie.

Millie blinks. Slow. As if her eyelashes are scared to meet. That smile. As if cut from a magazine and pasted on.

The SUV's brake lights flash. Natalie thumps her brakes to keep from rear-ending them.

The camera pans out. The little girl wears the Camp Zoom

T-shirt that arrived two weeks ago in a bubble-wrapped envelope. Millie packed it to keep from wearing it before the first day. Even if I see it, Ma, I'll wanna wear it. Nat packed the rest, following the typed list enclosed with the shirt, stopping only at feminine hygiene products. She hadn't considered it a possibility until now, but Millie's body might have, so she grabbed a handful of tampons from the restroom. MO-OM! Millie moaned, a pillow over her face. Just in case, Mill. You know how to use them? MOM! Well, read the directions if you don't. You can read? Then Millie giggled her hands-over-mouth giggle that she'd kept since she was two.

A person walks into the frame wearing the Camp Zoom T-shirt. Back to the camera and facing the sitting Millie. Only Millie's legs and arms are visible. Her hands dangle limply at her knees. Natalie zooms in on the ring on her finger. It flashes blue in Natalie's mind. As blue as it was when Millie shook it in the quarter machine plastic bubble. It's a sapphire like my birthday!

The SUV turns left at the junction. Natalie doesn't stop at the sign.

The screen goes black.

Then lights back up.

Millie is belly down on a bed covered in the sleeping bag she decorated with glow-in-the-dark fabric paint so it'd look new. A figure stands next to her. *Turn the radio up for that sweet sound, Ma*. Natalie slaps at the volume knob and then remembers how to use it. A voice fills the car. The voice is familiar. *A motel room is a motel room, right, folks?* Natalie groans, thumping her head against the headrest.

Dear Mom, the voice says, Camp's great, I'm having so much fun.

The camera moves down Millie's back. Her waist. Her underwear. (I'm too old for cartoon panties, Mother.) Her thighs painted with –

Not blood, not blood. Chocolate syrup like the *Psycho*

shower scene. Please, let it be chocolate syrup.

I'm learning lots of stuff, the voice says.

The backs of her knees –

Her right knee with a little cut from shaving too fast –

Her calves.

The speakers rattle. But it's lights out soon, the voice says.

Not yet! Natalie yells, keeping right behind the SUV. The interstate comes into view.

Her left ankle bound with a black shoelace. Her right ankle bound with a black shoelace.

Right bedpost.

Left bedpost.

P.S., the voice says, Don't come early.

I'm, Millie's voice breaks through, right as –

The screen goes black.

The radio shorts out.

Natalie smashes the heel of her palm against the radio again and again again again the crunch of her bone shoots around her body and out her mouth. MILLIE!

Natalie tries to shift with her broken hand then uses her left. She must pull the SUV over and ask where they got that movie, how it was even possible. She pulls her hazard lights. They don't blink. She leans against her horn. A thick sigh wheezes out. The window crank snaps off in her hand. Pull over, pull over!

The SUV turns right up the ramp. The Yugo coughs. Nat shifts down. A Camero refuses to move into the passing lane, so the SUV has to slow to merge. Nat catches up just in time to see the woman who drowned her children walking out of a courthouse and signing the book she wrote and Nat read. The SUV speeds off, passing the Camero on the right and moving into the left lane. Natalie swallows. She never noticed the license plate.

She looks over at her purse, her brother's cell phone that he insisted she take. Who do you call? Mom and Dad, long time no hear. I'm on my way to pick up Millie from camp and guess what. You won't, so go buy a helicopter at Wal-Mart and get here quick. Double-time it, Daddy-o. Before it's too late. Too late for what?

Calm down. You just imagined it all. Your very expensive imagination. But why would a farmer living on the outskirts of Charleston, Illinois have a video of Millie? Well, why not? Every dump-dive town had an adult bookstore. Even Millie knew that. For years she asked why they never shopped at that bookstore by the interstate. And there was the internet. She'd seen the TV program about dangerous websites, hidden cameras catching men walking into houses where fourteen-year-old girls supposedly waited.

Maybe it was a hallucination. Her hand yells that hallucination it most certainly was not. She glances at the envelope in the ashtray. The postmark says it was sent not from Bloomington, but Casey. Last Saturday. But camp didn't begin until Sunday. Millie dated the letter Monday night. Unless Millie wrote the letter in advance. Nat cries. But. Learning *stuff*. Having *fun*. Nat thought excitement kept Millie from details. She thought Millie would fill her in at the diner before she fell asleep on the ride home.

Nothing was strange about the postcard Nat tore from a poster in the art room while sweeping. It looked like every other art school poster with collaged pictures, muted colors. She left it on the kitchen table, thinking it would be nice next year after they saved money. But Millie filled out the card and dropped it in the mailbox. A heavy silver envelope arrived a week later. Natalie suddenly imagines a man in a dark office holding a black phone and dialing number after number from a list of 500. Hello, Lindsay, Hello, Jenny, Hello, Amanda, Peggy, Beth, Millie. This is the director of Camp Zoom and I'm happy to say you've won the number-one scholarship to attend film camp for free! A whole chorus of little girls screams Yippee!! then packs tampons in suitcases. At least, she didn't leave Millie alone when they arrived before the other campers. Millie had wanted her to. I'm not like other parents, she told Millie.

⋆══◉   ◉══⋆

The Camp Zoom signboard is unlit. All the motel doors are shut.

Natalie gets out of her car. The other parents will arrive soon. Maybe after similar journeys behind SUVs, maybe a few driving SUVs and wondering why the kiddies in the back seat are crying to turn it off – turn it off – off – .

There is not one giggle or girl. An empty movie set. She wants to call Millie's name, but the answer will be her own voice. Quit it, Nat. You saw nothing. You heard nothing. If you'd taken the whole day off instead of working at the school and the factory, your brain wouldn't be rigged for dreams.

She climbs the stairs Millie dragged her suitcase up six days ago. She finds Millie's door. Her good hand wraps around the knob. It clicks. The sound of tires on gravel whirls Natalie's eyes over her shoulder. A brown mini van parks in the space in front of the motel room where that daughter has lived for a week. Lived, Natalie whispers. The van door slides open.

Natalie steps into Millie's room.

Another vehicle pulls in.

Millie's suitcase is by the door, its end crumpled. Black streaks and tiny dents cover the inside of the door. No one checked to see which way the hinges sat.

A motel room is a motel room, right, folks?

Two beds. In the far one is Millie, belly-down on her sleeping bag.

More vehicles arrive, the engines ticking as the cars settle down.

Mothers and fathers walk on the balcony and below. One after another hotel door clicks open.

Mother after mother begins to scream.

69

Digging

Mother says to my brother, Go play outside.

My brother says, But there aren't any children left.

Mother says, Stay out of the forest or you will get lost. My eyes can't see far. Stay in the backyard.

My brother obeys, screen door banging behind him. I start to follow.

No, Mother says. Stay and help me bake a cake for your brother. My fingers are crooked from age and cannot grasp well.

Why are we baking a cake?

Tomorrow is his birthday.

But he is not to eat sugar or his pancreas will die.

I am his mother. Tomorrow is his birthday. It will be a special day and so he can eat sugar. Crack those eggs. Add them to the mixture.

I do.

Check the oven to see if it is hot enough.

It is, Mother.

She slides the cake pan into the oven. She sits at the kitchen table and falls asleep because she is very old.

I run outside.

My brother calls my name.

I follow my name to him.

He stands at the edge of the forest. His face is blank, unblinking. Like one of my dolls. I do not like my dolls because they ask questions I have no answers for. Like, who carved our pretty wooden doll beds? Or, what is that booming in the distance?

He points.

A shovel leans against a tree. Beside the blade is earth and roots. The roots like Mother's fingers. The earth is piled. Two holes. Very deep. I can't see the bottoms.

70

My brother asks, What do you see?

Someone's been digging.

Indeed, he says. My brother says indeed instead of yes. He reads many books.

Have you been digging, Brother?

No. What is our mother doing?

She is napping. A cake is baking because tomorrow is your birthday.

Tomorrow is not my birthday, he says. I will surely die if I eat that cake.

Mother said tomorrow is special so sugar is allowed.

I look into the holes. What do you bury in holes so deep? I ask.

Bodies, my brother says. He walks into the forest. Bring the shovel, he says. I do. It is tall and heavy.

We walk deeper. My brother raises his hand. He takes the shovel. He digs. He wipes his forehead with his sleeve.

That is not good manners, I say.

He climbs into the hole. He climbs back out, a dress in his arms. Do you remember our sister? he asks.

Yes. She combed my hair one hundred strokes before bed. She left for school in the city.

My brother lays her on the ground. Her dress faded pink. He digs into the other pile.

These are very fresh, he says.

He climbs in and out.

Do you remember our brother? he asks.

He carried me on his back like a horse. He left to open a business in the city.

My brother lays our brother next to our sister in the faded dress.

We walk further. My brother digs. Do you remember our other sister?

No.

She sewed your baby clothes. She told me fairy tales.

Mother said she ran away.

My brother props her against a tree. She has two brown braids. Her eyes are large and dark.

My brother digs.

This must be Father, he says, peering into the hole. This hole is deeper than the others. He climbs in. He weeps. He hugs the bones. The bones crumble. He screams.

Why are you screaming? I ask.

Leave me, he says.

No. I ask my sister for her leg. A moth winks in her eye. Thank you, I say. Then I hold her leg over the hole.

Take this, I say to my brother.

I wave it around in case his eyes are getting bad like Mother's. Take this and climb out, I say. He does. We give our sister back her leg.

Our mother calls our names.

My brother says, Our mother is old.

Her glasses are very thick, I say.

Tomorrow is not my birthday. She will tell you I am leaving for the city. This is not true. Do not tell her what we found.

Blankets are piled in the wheelbarrow so we drag our sister who left for school and our brother who left for business back to the house. They lose a few bones. Their hair drags. We are out of breath. We take them to our room and dress them in our clothes. They lean against each other in the closet as we sleep.

In the morning, Mother calls our names into the kitchen. We follow. Every counter is full of chocolate, gumdrops, small cakes. The biggest cake is yellow and on the table. Mother sings Happy Birthday.

Wish your brother a happy birthday, she says.

What if it isn't his birthday?

Brother kicks me under the table.

Why would I bake a cake if today wasn't? Mother says.

I shrug.

Mother slices two pieces onto our plates. Eat.

My brother says, I can't have sugar.

This is your special day, our mother says. You have my permission.

We pretend to eat the cake. We hide each bite in our pockets.

My brother says, I wish our brother and sisters were here to celebrate. And Father.

Our mother's shoulders shake. She says, I thought you'd forgotten. You never ask about them.

You told us where they went, my brother says. We believed you.

Our mother says, You are old enough to know now. And your sister is young enough to forget. You have heard me speak of the war.

My brother nods so I do too.

It came to the city. They died. They are buried in the forest.

But what about Father? my brother asks.

He died of sadness.

We are sleepy, Mother, my brother says. I must rest before I go to the war.

She follows us to our bedroom. She tucks us in. She shuts the door. Her footsteps go back to the kitchen. We roll out of bed and carry our brother and sister from the closet. We tuck them in. We kiss their foreheads. Then we hide in the closet. Our mother returns and leans over our bed. She clutches our wrists. She holds a mirror over our mouths. She leaves then wheels in the wheelbarrow. She picks us up. You are so light, she says. We follow her into the backyard. To the edge of the forest. She carries us into the holes with deep bottoms. Then she shovels earth over us. We do not protest. She sings Happy Birthday. We hear bombs. She apologizes for not singing a better song. She sits between us all through the night.

Park

I am ten and a half. My parents are neither dead nor divorced. My grandparents live next to us. They are my mother's parents. My father's parents are dead, and we live in their house where my father grew up. Grandmother sneaks me a peppermint pattie from her housecoat when I hug her. Grandfather offers me ice cream cones. I never say yes. Ice cream goes straight to the hips. This bathing suit is the color of my grandmother's turquoise ring. Mom says that when my grandfather is dead, I will regret never eating the ice cream.

Don't touch me. I don't like to be touched.

I like visiting the graveyard across the street and subtracting the tombstone's birth from death. That is why I am the best subtracter in my grade. My favorite grave is for a girl my age who died in 1878. An angel crouches on her tombstone, her wings spread, as if ready to fly Ruby away.

I haven't any siblings and don't wish for any. Children make me nervous. There aren't any in our neighborhood because all the ones Father grew up with got out of this godforsaken city. I don't like school, so Father puts Friday gifts under my pillow so I can make it through the week.

But my parents don't give me too much or too little. They are good, and I tell them so every night before I say the Lord's Prayer. One time my mom and I accidentally checked out an adult book on witches that was misplaced in my section of the library. There were black and white pictures of women standing on bundles of tree branches. We learned that beauty marks were once thought to be the devil's mark. We also learned that some people were killed if they messed up while saying the Lord's Prayer. My mother and I have lots of beauty marks. A stupid girl in my class said that my mother's beauty marks were chicken pox, but they aren't. They're dark freckles. But I have memorized the Lord's Prayer in case the stupid

74

girl in my class becomes a stupid adult and rises all the other stupid adults with her and they pick out a tree for my neck. I memorized it backward and forward so that if I make a mistake on purpose, it will seem accidental.

Once my parents are asleep after arguing, I turn my lamp back on so Ruby won't walk across the street and kill me for living. I would if I were her.

When my parents argue, my mom goes out back and smokes cigarettes. I can smell them in her hair when she comes back inside and tells me everything's all right and they love me very much.

Sometimes, I pretend I'm Ruby and that I am sleeping beside me. I tell me about my coffin and how dark it is and how a girl visits me, and she talks to me or brings over a checkerboard and pretends we're playing. I tell me that I should like living more and that the dark and silence aren't as wonderful as they sound, even if you hate hearing your parents argue. I tell me I can say anything since I don't have anyone to listen. When I'm Ruby, I'm glad not to be in the ground anymore. But she can't grow up, so I don't know what to do next year when I'm older than her.

Maybe next year I'll start looking like the girls who wear bikinis and kiss boys in the corner of the pool where the lifeguard can't see. Mom only lets me wear one pieces because bikinis are useless, and I'm not at the pool to pose for a magazine. You'd have to smile for that, anyway, she said.

I'm sad a lot. When I am, I pull my hair until I hurt more than sadness.

Please. I don't like to be touched. Please. Keep your hands to yourself.

I live on Linwood Avenue. It's a nice neighborhood with huge trees that hang over the street. All the houses have gardens, and every morning the old women wear straw hats and bend over their peonies and roses. Blue periwinkle spreads across our backyard. In the summer, men light fireworks that burn colors into the sidewalks. I wish we had a dog to walk, but I also wish for a beautiful tombstone so children will visit me and wonder who I was. Ruby had wishes. I wish she'd be my age next year.

When Mom asked what I do in the graveyard all afternoon, I told her about Ruby. I knew I shouldn't have because Ruby is mine. But Mom took me to the library. We looked at old newspapers on a screen. We found the one Ruby was in. She died of measles. Lots of people died of them because there wasn't a cure. We found Ruby's mother in another newspaper. I already knew about her because she's beside Ruby. She was a loving mother. Mom read me that she died of tuberculosis. Mom says my great-grandmother also died that way. Ruby's mother died thirty years after Ruby. Mom says the worst thing imaginable is for a child to die before its parents. I didn't tell her how I think about it. How I imagine myself hanging like a beautiful witch from the magnolia tree in the front yard. How I'm wearing the white satin nightgown I saw in the department store display window.

I also don't tell her about my nightmares anymore because they have gotten worse. In one, I fall backwards into an ocean and sink and sink and all I see is murky water and my hair floating out in front of me like periwinkle. There are sharks and they're coming after me. If I wake before the sharks rip me to pieces, I run to the bathroom and hold my head under the tub faucet until my head burns like the center of the earth. Do you ever know what you'll dream before you fall asleep? I mean, really know? The sharks will swallow me tonight.

I can't go on a vacation with you, and Mom won't let me because we are going to Shawnee soon. My dad wanted to name me Shawnee because a glacier carving out a forest is as amazing as birth. But Mom said be practical. My dad is rarely practical. He wants to quit his job and move out West. His van has a tent inside it and a first-aid kit and a fishing pole and a gun and a life jacket and binoculars. When I look through the binoculars, I always forget to hold them away from my face so my eyelashes brush the lenses and make everything blurry.

Where are we going? The mechanic is the other way. Mom will be mad at you if you don't take me there like you said she said. Turn around. She does not like unpunctual people! Turn around!

My dad will come after you when he finds out. He's taller than a house. He'll stomp you to bits.

Please. That hurt me.

Yes, my dad, my father ... he hates his job. He draws pictures of pipelines, but he'd rather draw something else. He was a painter when he met Mom. His paintings are stacked against a wall in the attic. He used to paint women. He says the paintings are off-limits, but when he's at work and Mom's lonely and sitting on my bed, I sneak up there and set the canvases on the floor beside each other. The women don't smile. Most of them aren't wearing clothes. The shadows across their cheekbones and down their thighs are bluish-green like bruises. The women tell me what my father used to be like. Very dashing. Funny. Rarely sad. He paints only landscapes now. When he takes me to the library, we sit in the adult section and look through the art books. I'm going to give a speech for 4-H about Van Gogh. He cut off his ear and gave it to a woman. He was sad. He shot himself in a field and walked home. There is a field behind the graveyard. My father takes many walks.

His paintings are probably worth money. Take me home, and he'll give you some, or I can sell them and give you the money. I'll leave it by Ruby's grave. I can leave some flowers on her grave so you'll find her quicker. Her only flowers are the ones blown from other graves.

Ruby was in the newspaper, but I'll only be in it if I get married, die, or have a baby. One birthday someone might put a younger picture of me in the community news as a surprise.

If you just let me out here, I can walk home. I know the way. I can see The Executive Inn in the rearview mirror. That's where my grandparents' anniversary was. There's a glass walkway that bridges over the street. They have a swimming pool. I know because after everyone was done eating, they sat around talking, so I went and rode the elevator. I got off at every floor and ran up and down the carpeted hallways. They all looked the same except a few doors had silver dinner plates in front – some of the plates still had food on them, beautifully scrumptious cheesecake with cherry sauce. I didn't eat any because I was tempted. After I ran around, I took the elevator to the next floor. An old man got in and said, Lobby, please, so I pushed the L button, and he gave me a quarter.

My future? Nothing grand. I'll probably teach first grade like my mother. And when my students grow up, I'll teach their children. Sometimes, I won't recognize them as adults when they see me in the grocery store, but they'll forgive me.

You have to take me back because this Sunday is communion, and if I don't forgive my trespasses, I'll go to hell. We also forgive those who trespass against us. I pray for Ruby. I can pray for you. I used to pray for Father, but he's still sad and unfolds maps of the West after dinner. During the sermon, I count the wood planks in the ceiling. I lose count around eighty. I'm too old to sing in the children's choir but too young to sing in Mom's choir. This little light of mine is my favorite song. Hide it under a bushel – no!

I will marry a good man. I will not love a man who is an artist and loves the sky more than me. I will not sit on my daughter's bed and forget she's there while I wait for the man I would have married if I hadn't married the boy next door. When my husband and I argue, I won't slam doors, and he won't leave inside-out volcanoes in the walls. I'll go sit in the bathroom with the door locked so my daughter won't wake up and hear and wish she could run out of her room and scream at them to quit it. Stop lying and just quit it!

I don't want children at all because maybe I will be an artist and get out of this godforsaken city. If I have children by accident, they will want to swim in the hot summers, and what if I don't want to drop them off at the public pool just because that's what the other mothers do?

If a day does come when I leave my daughter for just an hour because I have to find my husband because maybe he's left for the West, I will tell her not to take peppermint patties. I will tell her that my car tire won't go flat. I will tell her not to walk around the swimming-pool fence to a brown car. She won't feel the cold air cling to her turquoise bathing suit until it's too late. Until the man forces her to talk about herself.

All I Have Left

Alice and her goat follow the tracks up the dirt path to the old road.

She looks both ways. She looks at the goat.

You are all I have left, she says.

The goat cocks its head, blinks eyes black as asphalt.

Alice turns back down the path to the farmhouse.

The goat follows her to the porch where Mother sat during storms before she got sick. The storm blowing the wind chimes in every tree. The sound like Mother's silver bracelets colliding as she shut Alice's bedroom door for the last time.

Alice walks to the largest tree. She pulls herself onto the goat's back and grabs a tree limb. She climbs up and hangs upside down by her red stockinged knees, hair curling flat to grass.

Mother! she calls.

Mother, I can stay like this forever! she calls.

The goat grazes by the tree.

Alice swings back and forth. A bat flies over. Alice closes her eyes. She is a bat hanging from her bedroom ceiling. She sees a little girl in bed. A woman in a green skirt. The woman's black hair hangs around her face. For nine months you floated in light, says the woman.

Alice opens her eyes.

A boy stands there.

She falls out of the tree, bark grating the backs of her legs.

Your mother is dead, the boy says.

Who are you?

The boy looks past her to the house. You need to leave, he says. The villagers are coming.

I'll hide.

The boy strokes the space between the white goat's eyes.

He presses his thumb there. They'll kill your goat, he says.

Alice slaps his hand and pushes her skull against the goat's skull. It's all I have left, she says.

He shrugs. A goat won't matter if you're dead.

No one would kill a little girl.

You may carry your mother's disease, he says.

She wasn't sick.

Water, he says. Water.

Are you thirsty?

The first test, the boy says. For now, you pass.

Go away, Alice says.

Then turn your back or you might cause me to hurt myself. You might be like the other children.

I'm not like other children, she says.

The boy holds out his arms, palms up. Scars up his forearms. His skin like fruit split from ripeness.

Alice steps back. Who did that to you?

He drops his arms. Me.

How?

With crushed glass, he says.

Alice stares at him.

He stares at her.

Why? she asks.

How do you feel when you hang from that tree very long? he asks.

Dizzy.

Do you then kick the tree for making you so?

No. I stand up.

Hurting myself is like standing up.

The boy waits.

Alice doesn't turn away.

The goat blinks.

Alice calls the goat to her. They walk into the house, screen door slapping behind them. The boy wobbles into the shade of the tree Alice fell from, one leg dragging behind him.

81

⋅━○　　○━⋅

The boy lived with his father above his father's store. His window overlooked the sidewalk where the girl and her mother spread their blanket of glasswares on market days. The sun through the glass and onto their skin. The girl touching the colors patterning her arms and shoulders while the boy imagined her fingers were his. Her very straight legs, his legs. Her mother, his mother.

His father says the boy was one of two babies. When the boy and the other baby were born, his mother saw his one healthy leg and the ugly, smaller one, and she ran away with the straight-legged baby.

On market days, he woke early and waited for the woman and girl to appear on the dirt path. When the two figures did not cross the bridge into his eyesight, he left his room. He found the mother slumped on the other side of the bridge, her mouth crying tears the color of his hair. His father found him sleeping in the dead woman's arms and hoped it was his wife come back.

⋅━○　　○━⋅

Alice peels off her red stockings. The skin on the backs of her knees sticks to the fabric and rips away in bits. Alice winces. She puts on a clean pair. She crawls into bed. The white goat hangs its head out the window.

Is he gone? Alice asks.

The goat flicks its tail.

No one will kill us, Alice says.

She looks around her bedroom. No bat hangs in the corner. She turns on the red lamp on her nightstand. Beside the lamp is a jar with bits of swirled glass at the bottom. She picks up the jar. Her hands are small. Child hands, she thinks. Not like Mother's. The red light through the glass bits throws patterns on Alice's face and dyes the goat's fur pink.

The goat curls up next to her bed. Its eyes begin to shut, third eyelids moving in from the corners.

Alice drops her arm over the side of the bed and sinks her fingers in the goat's fur. She is always surprised at its coarseness. She suspects that most pets have soft fur. Mother didn't allow her to have a pet because when she was Alice's age, her father shot her dog. Mother says you could tell the dog was sick by its eyes. As if drilled into its head. Mother says she never thought she'd cry that much again until Alice's father died.

Alice shakes the jar. The sound like fairies hammering glass.

Maybe you don't miss your mother, Alice says to the goat, because you never knew her before she died. Like me and Father. But maybe you don't miss her because no one told you about her. I'll tell you what I know. Then we'll feel the same.

Alice sets down the jar. She kneels on the floor by the goat, her head on its belly.

Once upon a time when the next day was spring, Alice says, Mother was blowing glass in the shed. It was night. She heard a noise like an animal was hurt. She kept working because you'll ruin the glass if you stop in the middle. But the cry didn't stop and Mother started imagining bats eating cows or dogs without heads. So she took her flashlight outside, over the fence and into the field where a goat lay swollen. The goat was your mother and you were the baby inside. Mother sat with her all night, until you tumbled out, bloody sac of hooves and hair. Then your mother died and my mother buried her. In the morning, I came down for breakfast. Mother sat at the kitchen table with you in her arms. Her arms and hair stuck with blood from the night before.

⊷═◉   ◉═⊷

Out back, the boy sits in the glass wading pool Alice's mother made.

83

You're still here, says Alice.

I slept under the bridge in case you tried to go into the village to find your mother. And, in case someone left the village to find you.

They won't find me.

They know the direction you walk from on market day. They know who you are. The glass girl. Alice, he says.

You know my name, she says.

It was the last word your mother said before she died.

Maybe she said glass, Alice says.

Maybe, he says. But I heard it before she said it.

You are the devil.

No.

Take me to her, Alice says.

She's buried.

We'll unbury her. Just like Mother said she'd unbury the goat.

Another goat? the boy asks.

My goat's mother, Alice says. Mother told me not to follow her into the field, so I watched from my bedroom window.

What did she do? the boy asks.

She just sat out by where it was under the earth.

What happened to your father? he asks.

He's dead.

I'm sorry.

Don't lie.

I'm not. My mother is dead probably, too.

I don't care about your mother, Alice says. Tomorrow is market day. Take me to see mine.

That isn't a good idea.

The villagers won't kill me. They bought Mother's glass art. They display her vases and lamps in their windowsills.

Not anymore, the boy says. My father found her and carried her to the village. The villagers saw why she died. They broke the glass and melted it with your mother's body.

Alice looks at the boy. The wading pool water evaporates, air rippling between them.

They burned her, Alice says.

He nods.

Alice bites her lip.

They melted her like hot glass, Alice says. Alice goes to the boy. She kneels by the wading pool and touches one of the boy's scars. If you had a mother, she wouldn't have let you do this.

He slaps her hand away.

She smiles. Your hair is the color of the blooms that fall from the tree in the front yard, she says. This is my house and my yard.

The boy says, How did your father die?

Alice says, He turned into a flower.

The goat's hind leg buckles.

⋯⧯⟩   ⟨⧯⋯

Alice hangs from a tree branch. Look, Mother, she says, I can stay here forever!

Mother tickles her belly.

Alice giggles, as she will the night Mother leaves after telling the glass story. After Mother stands by the door, eyes sweeping the walls, the floor, the red lamp, Alice will ask what she's doing and Mother will say, making a memory. Then Alice will call her a silly Mother and giggle.

Alice's hair swings ahead of her body.

You might get hungry if you hang there forever, Mother says.

You'll bring me food, Alice says.

Are you a goat? You'll have to eat upside-down.

I'm no goat! Alice laughs.

You aren't? Mother runs her fingers through the wind chime hanging by Alice's head. The sound like fairies hammering glass. Are you a wind chime?

85

No, Mother. I'm not made of glass anymore.

If you hang there forever, I'll have to go to market alone.

You can take my goat, Alice says.

Mother taps her bottom lip. It might rain while I'm gone. The goat can keep you company, but it can't hold an umbrella.

I'll call your name, Alice says.

I'll be too far away to hear.

Then I'll wave my hands like this, Mother. Watch, Mother. I'll wave my hands like this and you'll hear me like a bat. I'm a bat, Mother!

Mother stops smiling. The dog bit at the bite on its leg. The bat's bite. The dog chewing its leg to the bone, snapping at its death.

Get down from there, Alice.

But I'm not dizzy yet.

Now.

⇢═◉   ◉═⇠

Alice turns her back to the boy and says to the goat, Come here, all that I have left.

The goat doesn't.

Alice carries a bucket to the well. She cranks the knob. She used to pretend the water was hot glass and her fingers were made of metal. Her mother sculpted glass. She winces.

What's wrong? the boys asks.

Nothing. Alice calls again to the goat. It doesn't come.

You need to drink, Alice says.

The goat blinks eyes black as Mother's hair.

Drink, Alice says. She nudges the bucket with her foot, water sloshing.

The goat whines. It backs up. Dust at its hooves.

Stop acting like Mother, Alice says.

What'd you just say? the boy asks.

Nothing.

Tell me.

I'd rather strangle myself with red stockings, Alice says.

⊷═◌   ◌═⊷

Mother lay in bed, her arms raised like a goat dead for several days. Outside, Alice plays in the wading pool, water rainbowing in splashes. Alice pretends the water is molten glass. She sticks her fingers through the prisms.

All Mother can think of is her dog. Mother knows the symptoms. She looks at her arms. As a child, she stood by the tilting porch as the family dog bit its back leg. Father knotted a rope around the dog's neck then disappeared into the field.

She cries. Tears lock her throat.

She hooked her hands in Father's back pockets, her feet like hooves stuck in the dirt. She shouted at her dog to scram – get away – not safe. But the dog only turned. Eyes dead and unblinking. Then her fingers slipped from her father's pockets. Get on back to your mother, Father said. Don't follow, Father said. She snapped beans on the porch until he walked back with the twilight, gun, sack, and shovel. What's in the bag, Daddy? A surprise for me, Daddy? He shook his head, tossed the sack in the barn, pulled the door shut. Time for bed, sugar. She waited for dark and his snores. Then she sneaked to the barn. She untied the sack. Stuck in her arm.

Wet fur.

Teeth.

⊷═◌   ◌═⊷

Alice runs into the house, hands cupped in front of her. She slips over the linoleum in stockinged feet.

Mother! she calls. Water drips from the spaces where her fingers meet.

I have a surprise for you!

Alice follows the feeling of Mother upstairs. Mother is in bed, scratching at her arm.

Why are you scratching like that? asks Alice.

Mother makes sounds in her throat.

I can't hear what you're saying, Mother. You need to open your mouth.

Mother shakes her head, her black hair catching in her eyelashes.

Are you drooling bubbles again, Mother? asks Alice.

Mother nods, weeping.

Alice sets her surprise in the water glass on the nightstand and picks up the towel. She wipes Mother's eyes. Open your mouth, Mother.

Mother pushes her head back into the pillow and moans.

Please, Mother.

Mother opens her mouth.

Alice wipes Mother's lips.

Do you want to see your surprise now? Alice picks up the water glass and holds it in front of Mother's face. A ladybug floats there, black legs pulled into black undershell.

Mother pushes to the other side of the bed.

Don't you like your surprise, Mother?

Dump it. Get rid of it. Please, Alice.

Are you feeling worse, Mother? Your eyes are so big and black.

⤜⬤   ⬤⤛

The goat runs in circles.

Your goat is sick, Alice.

Don't say my name.

You must kill it.

Go home.

I don't have a home, says the boy.

You're from the village. Your father owns the store where we sell on market days. You live in the room above the sidewalk. I saw you in the reflection on the glass vases.

I'm not from the village anymore, he says. You must kill

88

it. Then we'll go get help.

From the villagers who want to kill me? asks Alice.

From a doctor.

I'm not sick.

The villagers say the sickness is incurable if you wait too long. You will not feel sick until too late. Like your mother.

She only had a sore throat.

Then why did she leave?

She's coming back, says Alice.

She's dead.

Alice runs to the goat and throws her arms around its neck. She weeps like Mother after Alice asked for the glass story. Mother rocking her forehead against Alice's.

Get away from the goat, he says.

It's all I have left.

He moves toward her, his body shifting back and forth, his lame leg trying to keep up. He holds out his arms. You have me, he says.

Alice narrows her eyes. I don't want you! You're a cripple. No one wants a cripple.

His face burns red as stockings. He falls next to the water bucket. He shoves his head in the bucket and grips the sides, his fingers white with the pressure. White as blossoms.

Stop it! she yells.

His body bucks like the goat will when the sickness is ripe in its brain.

I'm sorry, Alice says. I didn't mean it. She takes two steps forward.

He goes limp.

Alice kicks the bucket. The metal cuts into his cheek. He falls, water and vomit bubbling in his mouth. His mouth shaping a word like glass or Alice.

You're alive, she says.

Alice, he says. He looks at the water speckling her arms. You pass again, he says.

89

The goat pulls its frozen hind leg into the shade of a tree.

-→━○　　○━←-

The night Mother leaves, Alice lays in bed. The white goat at Mother's feet. Mother's hands tremble. She must leave – she scratches at her arms – because maybe Alice doesn't have it.

You don't look well, Alice says.

Mother tries a smile. I'm well enough to tell you a bedtime story before I go to the doctor.

Alice smiles. She leans back onto the pillow. The pillow is cool like Mother's hands during storms. All night Alice will move her cheek from one side of the pillow to another.

What story tonight? asks Mother.

Alice taps her finger on her lip like Mother when she's thinking hard. She looks at the jar of swirled glass on the nightstand.

Tell me why the fairy leaves glass under my pillow when I lose teeth.

Mother picks up the jar as if weighing a vase's price before selling it at market.

Well, says Mother, she doesn't leave glass. She turns your teeth back into glass.

Alice rolls onto her side. Mother's hair hangs like black paint strokes on glass.

Do you want the short version or the long one? asks Mother.

Are you blowing tonight? asks Alice.

Mother looks at her hands on the jar of glass. She shakes her head. Not tonight.

Then the long version.

Mother weeps.

Did I hurt your feelings, Mother? I like the short version, too.

It's not that, Alice.

I could tell you the glass story, Mother. I've memorized it.

No. It is important that tonight I tell you the story. The glass story it is.

⇢⇒◎   ◎⇐⇠

Alice walks into the shed where Mother made glass in the nights while Alice watched from her bedroom. The light of the fire washing across Mother's face.

She wraps the vases in heavy cloth and packs them in the saddlebags. She packs a smaller set and hangs it over her shoulder. She calls the goat. It doesn't come. She walks around the house.

The boy stands by the tree that blooms blossoms the color of his and Alice's hair. The blossoms that shed from the trees during storms. He stands next to the goat. The goat is tied to the branch Alice hung upside down from. Its eyes wide and black.

Untie all that I have left, Alice says to the boy. I am going to the village to see where my mother is buried. To see if what you say is true. Untie all that I have left.

The boy and goat shake their heads. It has the disease, he says. You must kill it or let it die here.

UNTIE ALL THAT I HAVE LEFT! screams Alice.

The boy goes to her, one foot bumping against the ground. He touches her shoulder like he imagined from his bedroom window. He watches his hand reach to touch her. His fingers glance off her skin. She snaps at his hand, tiny teeth snagging flesh.

His hand whips back.

He looks at his hand the same way Mother held out her arms and remembered the goat's blood smearing her arms and hands as she helped it birth.

He clutches his hand to his chest. Blood the size of ladybugs crawls into the punctures.

91

The body is a blown glass globe of light, Mother says. For nine months, you floated, suspended by silk from the balcony of your mother's brain. Your name will be Alice. Alice. Every night the moths rocked you between their wings. The fairies were so jealous that they flew with their hammers to crack the globe. Armies of fairies arrived all night with pebbles and picks and storms. Finally, you hatched from the blown glass. I found you at the foot of the old tree and wrapped you in flesh to keep you from breaking. But your teeth are bone and your bones are glass.

Mother leans over Alice, hair curling flat to Alice's bare arms. She pulls the sheet to Alice's chin. Then she stands up and looks around the room.

What are you doing? asks Alice.

Making a memory.

You're a silly Mother, says Alice. Then she giggles.

I have to go to the village. To see the doctor.

You are dying, Alice says.

Maybe, Mother says.

Like Father?

I might be dead like Father, but I am not dying like Father.

I don't have any pictures of you, Alice says.

You have the pictures of your father. And when you are older, all you must do is look in a mirror. Then look at your father and subtract him from what you see.

Mother moves to the bedroom door, her silver bracelets sliding down her arm.

Mother?

Yes?

Don't die.

My mother wasn't sick! Alice yells.

The boy holds his damaged hand.

She had a sore throat! Alice yells. She coughed! I felt her head! She was going to feel better in the morning!

The boy looks at Alice.

And I sat by her bed and watched. I cleaned her mouth. When she woke up, she went out in to the field where the mother goat was buried. I followed, but she said, no, Alice go home. Alice go away.

Go away, Alice, the boy says.

The goat stands like a mother about to die of the sickness. Body rigid, neck at the wrong angle.

Alice looks at the boy's hand.

She looks at her goat.

At the house.

At the path that will take her to the bridge and into the village or away from the village.

Rabbits

Nurse says I cannot leave the darkened room. She says I have the measles and could go blind if I see the sun. She says blind is like the dark. But Nurse lies. Everyone knows when you stare into the sun, it traps inside your eyes and all you see is light. Nurse touches the drapes every time she's in the room. As if they'll fly open and blind me if she doesn't. Nurse says do not pull the golden drapery cord because behind the drapes is a large window that looks into the garden and sun.

I used to wish for my little brother to visit and peek through the drapes and tell me what is truly there because Nurse says there is a garden full of yellow and pink snapdragons and a little path where brown spotted rabbits jump and dance. But I don't wish for him anymore. He would be scared to come in here now. It is much darker.

Nurse pretends it is not so dark. I test her by asking for my little brother. Instead of saying he can't come because he's scared, she says he will get the measles. I laugh and say then he wouldn't be scared of the dark anymore. Nurse says I'm a cruel little girl to wish death on loved ones. She doesn't know I'm onto her game.

Nurse would win if my little brother were in this bed. He doesn't suspect that adults lie to children. That they lie because they miss playing tiddlywinks so they make up their own games, but you have to figure out the rules to beat them. Rules such as, there is a window and garden and sun. Rules such as, you will go blind. Don't pull the golden cord.

Nurse is afraid of losing, which is why she's stopped lighting the lamps. I pretend not to notice the dark. I'm not scared because I'm not my brother. She can't trick me.

My brother is so terrified of the dark that he hates to shut his eyes – even for sleep. That's why Nurse ties stockings around his head and lets him blame her for taking away the light. Nurse is very sly. Which is why she gives me a rabbit stuffed with stockings. She says I must be lonely without my little brother to play with. She says your rabbit is alive and wants to play in your bed-garden. I say rabbits in gardens might as well be dead since I can't see them. She says the drapes must stay closed and don't wish for death or blindness because measles can do both.

But she's lying about pulling the cord because she lies about rabbits. Stuffed rabbits don't become alive until children have loved them so much that their button eyes fall out and noses rub away. I don't tell Nurse about blindness and rabbits because she refuses to tell the truth about the window.

Nurse is losing because she didn't realize that turning out the lamps has caused great improvements in my hearing. I hear my brother's tin soldiers clack in war in the nursery. I hear my baby dolls' eyes open and shut. I hear Nurse's shoes creak around the house. When I hear my brother breathing, I yell and hit the wall because it's so dark I'm beginning to forget what light is. Nurse says be quiet. Nurse says loudness is not good for young ladies with or without measles. I ask if loudness is not good for ladies with or without sight. She says don't wish for bad things. I say I'm onto you.

I press the rabbit's eyes to mine and colors burst in my head. I ask the rabbit what it sees. It says the lamp is lit low.

I cannot love a rabbit that talks like Nurse. So I chew out its back seam and tie the stockings around my eyes.

When Nurse comes in, I say look I'm blind. All I see is dark and it's all your fault. Nurse gasps. She spanks me and says she won't describe the garden through the window anymore.

I laugh because she knows she's losing. She says wait until you're better and see for yourself Miss Impatience. She touches my forehead. Her fingers run through my hair. They sound like rabbits slipping on a frozen pond. I try to slap her hands away. She says don't act like you're blind. I ask if blindness is worse than lying.

Nurse says I can play in the garden tomorrow. I say like a rabbit stuffed with stockings?

She pretends not to understand because the game's about to finish. I explain she wishes me blind. That's why she gave me the rabbit. That's why she's stopped lighting lamps. She says the lamps are lit. I say sore loser. I know I can't play in the garden. I say do you mean the garden behind the window? She says of course. She says the sun can't hurt you now. I laugh very cruel and scream LIAR! Then I crawl across the carpet as if I'm blind. And I show her that there is no garden. No window. I pulled the golden cord. I saw.

Wednesday Night Reflections, Edited Thursday

You tell me that in ten years you will live in London. Greeting the man who sings arias while selling oranges at the London market.

Vision twirls like a fan blade. Due to light-mindedness, I give you my wineglass before climbing to the floor at your feet.

When we talk, you touch my thigh. You have done this from the first time we met. I have poems to prove this.

That summer in the room without windows, I wore a short skirt and forgot to cross my legs, you told me later, and although I was embarrassed, I enjoyed the secret.

My paintings hang on the walls, surrounding us. You like that they all resemble me. I like to think it's my martyred eyes.

Two chords strung down my cheeks. Jesus, how I cry after you leave.

After you get into your car, do you sit there and sigh or just reverse out of the parking lot?

You think Wilco is the sound of Chicago, and I agree, even though I no longer live there. You've even taken my streets, my homeless man in front of Blockbuster I took coffee to after I closed the store for the night.

You were taking me home, but you turned the other way at the traffic light and, for a second, I hoped you'd forgotten the destination, that you were taking me away from this sulfur city. But before I could make love to you in the forest, we were in the library's asphalt parking lot, dropping off your daughter's books. She ignores the text and makes up her own stories to fit the pictures.

As we contemplated our own sweat, you rested your head in the curve of my spine, and I said, He rests his head in the wheel of shadow. And you said, You are dangerous. I can't remember why I said that.

Your cheek hot against me, but I'm making up the heat because temperature rarely survives memory. I know that there were Tuesdays of winter coats and scarves and Tuesdays in flip-flops.

Each time I am with you.

It is difficult, impossible really, to watch us from a different perspective. To say, the girl with the martyred eyes is in love with the man who checks the weather in Tucson.

Is it wrong to make you my muse? My Tuesday lover?

I recall our conversations without silences. But there must have been. Your foot spanning my hipbones as I watched you talk.

You are the only one who kisses me and walks away slumped. It's painful to watch. Even though it's not because of the kiss. Soft mouths without language express exactly what we were avoiding.

You sang, "Jesus, don't cry" because you knew I did.

The shadow of your anklebone. The fine, black hairs on

your toes.

I put you to bed that night, helped you crawl onto the mattress. Folded your jeans. But maybe they were slacks because there was a belt that you forgot on my chair in the morning.

The nightmares of missing an article of clothing in public. The nightmares of a happier self.

No matter how much I diagram what we will say or how the shadows will cast our profiles as we talk, it's forgotten in the sound of your knock. You are the only one who forces me into present tense.

This time I thought I would kiss you immediately. Instead, I hugged and it felt false.

You say that you'll miss coming here. It doesn't make this any easier. My bruised shrine of women, their haunted eyes.

She tells him everything she's thought since they last saw each other. She collects her thoughts like dynamite and hires a guard with a pistol to keep any form of ignition away.

Kiss me before I ask.

Our intensity, the stride of our steps, even our names – it is hard to believe they are all the same. I no longer correct people who want to spell my name like yours.

It's in the sound.

We no longer laugh at the irony of homophone goodbyes.

It's taking longer to recover from your visits. Like my grandmother who must rest after the great-grandchildren visit and color on her floor and tell her knock-knock jokes and eat handfuls of M&Ms out of the green candy dish with the heavy lid. I told you how she puts stickers beneath her figurines so that when she dies they go to the right grandchild, and I said you could have it to use in one of your stories.

How can you not understand why? How can you expect me to find a language to explain?

I'm going to kiss you.

In New Orleans, a wild-haired man played rows of glasses with a fork.

Your hand baring my back.

Of course it's your eyes, the beauty mark aslant from your bottom lip.

That night I broke a wineglass and later spilled another. I forgot and lay horizontal, my hair soaking up the merlot – or was it cabernet that time? – and I knew I wouldn't wash it, that I'd keep it a secret and thrill over the dry ends the next day, my wine-dyed hair, as if you leaned my head over a sink and poured it over my head.

I left you there, sleeping.

You leave things at my apartment – CDs, books, your must-dusky scent that I imagine must be Arizona lingering – to ensure your return. I am your pawnshop, refusing to sell to another buyer. This can go on forever, like when I was little and it would take an hour to get home, even though I lived five minutes away from my best friend. I'd walk her home then she'd walk me home and this was repeated until one of our mothers said enough.

The heat of your palm.

If you want a plot, don't ask me.

Without images, I am nothing. Not even a story. It's impossible to have one when I only see you on Tuesdays. We are in the middle of it. And if I gave you a plot, it would be what I imagined.

We don't look any different to each other than we did five years ago. As if we were expecting sudden change, something to prove that it had been too long to pick back up. But we're the weekly Soap Opera with the same characters living the same day.

If we'd met now. If we'd met tomorrow…

No silence.

You sing on the el. It's hard to believe, but I must because I don't lie.

Translate me if you must know why.

Your other lives spiral around the sanctuary of bruised women. It's distressing to think of you with a life outside my apartment or backyard.

"Jesus, don't cry. You can come by any time that you want. I'll be around."

Do you remember when someone stole your bicycle seat, and

I gave you a ride? Or when you thought I wouldn't be able to open your CD player to see what the CD was, and I did, and it was Modest Mouse. Of course, Modest Mouse.

Why does his posture weep after kissing her?

A parable:
The lovers are meeting for the first time in twenty years. They've agreed on a diner with cracked red booths on the corner of North and Clark. He's on the #36, thinking of her. She's always early and so he knows she's already in the smoking section, pretending to ponder the menu but really pretending she's someone else and observing the woman's chewed fingernails. He gets off the bus. He's lighting a cigarette as he crosses the street. He sees her and is suddenly slammed by a car. Skull shattering with windshield and interior mirrors. She doesn't see any of this behind the menu. Although the sirens dredge the depths of her, she ignores the feeling, adds it up to anticipation. She thinks he stood her up. She chain-smokes the hurt.

Every Tuesday. Every Tuesday. Oh.

When you're in Chicago, I convince myself I don't love you, that I just enjoy conversation. I critique us like a bad short story. And then you're knocking and no longer can I believe my illusions. Terrible.

I am telling the truth, but I'll call this fiction because who would believe that lovers like us still exist? We are as fossilized as Lancelot and Guinevere. It's our bond, the way reality often supersedes fiction, and we're the only ones left to make fiction real, to give it a believable plot.

Boy meets girl. Boy touches her arm as he talks. He's the

first person to do this. She's stopped doing it herself because it makes people edgy. It's a gesture she learned from her mother.

Stop leaving your music here.

Across the lawn, the woman dyes her hair. She thinks she's forgotten her natural color, but as soon as it reappears, she cannot.

Puddles like bruises.
    All the Tuesdays become one.
    I left you sleeping and returned to cry in the bottom sheet's indentation. Searched the pillowcases for your scent. While I was gone, you returned for your belt.

The other men were sad attempts to hate you. We both try. You beg me to hate you, so that you can take your belongings home this time. The only good thing about Hubert Selby's short stories is that they brought you back. This may sound submissive, begging. A woman not strong enough not to care if her lover returns. This is just how it is. The games people play.

The length of our separation is equal to the number of wine glasses it takes to dizziness.

This all must seem idealized. It's not. I'll add to it: You're a Cancer, I'm a Virgo. We have a 54% chance at our relationship, based on numerology. My horoscope for the Monday you came over said it would be my best day in a very long time. It was.

I lied about why I slept with another lover and another and another. I never liked their writing, their different lives, their hoping I don't realize they'll leave me by morning. I undress them again and again because they are not you. I'm safe because I don't care; none can enter my mind through back-doors I've locked. Any of them.

You say my expression is harsh, unapproachable. It's abstract enough to warn potential trespassers of danger.

All your women are bruised.
    You are dangerous.
    Why?
    Jesus, don't cry.

I shouldn't be upset that you sleep with other women because we're not together. We do not say I love you, which might make this worse because of the silence where love should be – but there are no silences, right? Not in memory. We are a pawn shop. Actually, you never return what I lend. And I don't have the currency you accept.

The plot began with a short skirt and you across the room shuffling papers. Your hand on my thigh since then.

There are these panicked moments.

I thought my black hair dramatic, and although everyone else complimented me, once the black was gone, I believed only you. This is problematic, perhaps. Another safety on my toy gun.

It's easier to deny when only a centimeter of natural brown comes through.

While you were in the bathroom, the bartender asked if you wanted another glass of water. I said yes, the first time I've taken your voice or made you decide. I wanted to hug the bartender with the joy of it, dance him around the room.

With you, my language is flawed, susceptible. A turtle walking across the interstate.

Promise you will pose for me. To see if I bruise even you. I, with paint. You, with your mouth and the years I didn't know you in Arizona.

Because I watched you talk to her. I heard you comment on her beauty when she was gone. It should've been me you were talking about. Me!

This clenching.

I only ask because you won't.

Only you refuse me the right to be another character, and therefore throw me headlong into myself, expecting me to acclimate instantly.

In Chicago, I stood on the sidewalk across the street from American Girl, watching you above as you served tea to little girls, dolls, and mothers. We never met while I was there because of your schedule. Again. No matter. No matter, right?

If we entered wholly into our daily lives, it wouldn't work. To make this a comedy, I'd paint us in a kitchen with a vase of daisies on the table. As I cook breakfast, you hug me from behind, your shower-wet hair dripping down my neck. But it's tragedy. I want this and since you don't, I laugh. Pretend it's impossible.

Move with me. I'll buy the U-Haul. Move with me and be there when I wake up. I'll be quiet and creep around getting ready to go write at the diner. At the diner, I'll think of how you get out of bed and shuffle to the bathroom, tripping over my shoes. How you wait until you're dressed to look in the mirror, or maybe you don't. But you can't, and you won't meet me at any diner. You'll read my stories, but what's that mean? There is your daughter, there is London in ten years. But she could live with us in the summers. She could fly down once a month. I checked. The airport's not too far. Three cigarettes away.

Who else has loved the shadow of your anklebone?

The neighbors would hate us for not giving in to pleasantries as we unlocked our front door. We'd be the writers next door.

He checks the weather in Tucson.

I fear you're waiting for me to realize something, like a poem too aloof to be analyzed completely. I'm floundering here.

The horoscope said we won't end our relationship even if it's floundering. You say, Astrology is such a woman's creation. See me, I'm hanging up the stars right now. I'm hanging them just like your bathrobe and mine on the same hook. Knots of tissue balled in the pockets.

Skeletons/My Fourth Birthday/
Hell is Channel Three

Mother comes into my bedroom. She drops a black trash bag on my leg. Her feet are bare and tan, crisscrossed by sun. You're too old to play with stuffed animals now, she says.

She doesn't crouch, take my face into her dish-soapy hands. She doesn't say, Bring them back from their adventures first. She's already gone, perfume like Father's cigar smoke. The kitchen faucet water rushes through the pipes in the wall then stops. A plate slides in the drying rack. The faucet turns on – off – another plate.

Raggedy Andy is on my pillow, staring at the clothes-hanger paper mobile. He doesn't like it – how it begins turning without breeze. Hanging in prayer around my bedpost is the yellow chimpanzee I tried giving to my babysitter, but she said her stuffed animals went in her closet when she married. Father's closet is padlocked. The combination in his head in a helmet an ocean away. I've seen Mother turning the dial.

I shut the door. Father painted my room dark blue. He ran out in the upper right corner. The paint store was closed. In the morning, they took him back to where children turn into fireworks.

I open the trashbag.

I'll suffocate, Boxy the turtle says.

Mother found him in a booth in the diner. The same people drink coffee there every afternoon. They play board games. One man brings jolly ranchers to only the women and children. They melt the change together in Mom's apron, the car ashtray.

There's a TV in the corner of the diner like in the hospital room in Father's older letters. Mother watches for Father's face in the war footage on channel three. They all look the same, she says, squinting. She calls Grandmother from the diner to ask if that was him – channel three – a second ago – holding the hand of an arm torn from a child's body. All the bodies look the same, laundry bags full of flesh.

I line the animals against the wall. From one corner to the electric outlet. Their black glass eyes clink against the wall.

Father came home last July. I waited for dark with the brown paper bag full of sparklers. The park fireworks whistled. People clapped far away. Mother sat by Father on the front step. He was hunched over, ears between knees, her hand hovering above his back. Look! I said, holding my squirt-gun by my cheek, shooting so I looked like a fountain. She covered her eyes. I threw my gun at the sidewalk. He shook his head. Only one firework got above the trees. Red like Father's eyes in the photographs in Mother's closet.

I slide my squirt-gun from my mattress. The mold-line is super-glued. The white trigger jiggles. I aim at the back of Raggedy Andy's red yarn head. I fire. Until his head is heavy, drooping, forehead slumped to the carpet. I aim at the next head – the next – water gurgling through the trigger hole – the next – leaking into my hand – down my wrist.

I wrap the bodies in my pillowcase. I stick my arm in the trash bag. The plastic smells like the end of something. If I crawl all the way in, I'll end up on channel three.

Why Jimmy

O ff the record, Grandmother brought Jimmy to our house because his goodfornothing mother was hooked on the bad stuff which I should've understood because my mother is also a goodfornothing which is also why I live with the Grands.

For the record, now that Jimmy doesn't have feet he can't walk all over my books or jump on my coverlet, and *that* satisfies me greatly. He also can't stand on Grandmother's steamer trunk, which is why this whole ordeal began. Really, this can all be traced back to God because he created people and so he should be in jail instead of Grandfather. But I suppose that won't hold up in court so start with Jimmy's goodfornothing mother. Skip to his dragging Grandmother's steamer trunk and scratching the wooden floor, so that I had to pull the rug over the scratches. It was a trial to pull that rug.

If Jimmy's goodfornothing mother sent his birthday present in winter on his actual birthday, he wouldn't have a temptation to succumb to. But she sent it in summer and so Grandfather put the present on the high shelf for safekeeping. Maybe it's Grandfather's fault for not letting Jimmy open the present, but it's not his fault that Jimmy acts like his goodfornothing mother and Grandfather's willy-nilly son who got hisself locked up – have mercy! – and became Mr. Goodfornothing instead of Our Precious One, which is why Jimmy's mother became Mrs. Goodfornothing, seeing as how the woman takes her husband's name.

Well, Mrs. Goodfornothing forgot to put Jimmy's actual present in the box. Jimmy should have known the box was empty because he had been sending mind messages to his mother. According to Jimmy, the reception for mind-messages is better the higher up you are. Long story short, the roof was hotter than the concrete around the park swimming pool so we couldn't stay long. Maybe that's why Jimmy's mom only got the part about any old shoebox will do. But he said she had received his messages and that the present was a map to her house. He said the present came early because she wanted him to begin the long journey and arrive to her by the time of his actual birthday.

Off the record, I am not so easily convinced, but I also had a mother plan, and since no magicians are listed in the Yellow Pages, I had to place all my bets on Jimmy.

Jimmy learned about mind-messages from a book about a sad girl who moved objects with her mind. I had to swear on Grandmother's casket receipt that I wouldn't tattle because the Grands would not approve of adult books with scary covers. I swore, even though the kitty inside me thought I was not doing the Godly thing. While I was supposed to be looking out so the Grands wouldn't catch Jimmy and the book, I saw the neighbors pull a refrigerator box to the curb then drive off. I jumped out the window and ran quick so that if Jimmy called my name he'd end up tattling on hisself.

I dragged the refrigerator box between the garage and the fence where I go when I don't want anybody looking at me or asking me what's wrong. I fit perfect inside the box. Long story short, my thoughts and I agreed to make the box my own special house. If Mother got word I had a house of my own she'd step toe on my doorstep and finally know a good thing when she sees it. I'd give her a tour of my house, and after a quick game of Shoots and Ladders, we'd drive to the park.

She wouldn't sit on the playground bench with her Sunday crossword and get irate with me for asking her to underdog me in the swing because she's not a suffering old woman with arthritis and halitosis and liable to break a hip if I swing back and kick her with my feet even if it is by accident.

She'd push me in the swing – my back or the seat or the flats of my feet. And this time, she wouldn't go talk to the man at the fence then wander into the little wooden playhouse by the tall slide where teenagers write bad words in permanent marker on the walls and ceiling. And I will not sit at the window while he wraps his ugly belt around her thin arm, her arm like a cassette tape streaming black ribbon.

I drew windows on my new house and painted the inside with the yellow paint left over from the kitchen since Grandmother refused to die in a house with a white kitchen.

I would have come out the first time Grandmother called my name, but she sounded weak – like my mother when the man ribboned her arm – and that scared me. When Grandmother started singing the song that made the kitten inside me cry, I unhid myself. But the box taped itself to my shoe and followed me halfway to the porch. When she saw me and the refrigerator box, she called me by my whole name and said my whole name should know that there's no difference between acting like trash and being trash and did I want to grow up to be my mother?

The kitty chased its tail in circles in my belly until I felt dizzy, too.

So I started running in circles and shouting to keep from pushing her down. Then I was over her knees, getting a sound wallop that should teach me a thing or two about – I'm not quite sure exactly what word she said – probably respect.

If Jimmy hadn't laughed at me when I was back in my room then I wouldn't have kicked his dumb mouth. And his two front teeth, which weren't babies anymore, wouldn't have jumped into his windpipe and so he wouldn't have grabbed at his throat and started shaking and so I wouldn't have had to go get Grandfather. But he laughed so I kicked so he grabbed so I told Grandfather so I had to explain how this all began so Grandfather found out about me in the neighbor's trash.

After Jimmy coughed up his teeth and Grandmother made an appointment for the dentist who wants to send us to a poor house, Grandfather made us sleep in trashcans so we'd know what trash truly felt like. If we had not slept in trashcans in separate rooms, I never woulda remembered how peaceful my own place felt.

Nice. It felt nice.

But then Grandmother died and so all the catalogs by the toilet for rainy, paper-doll days stayed where they were and she got buried in the casket named August Bloom. Grandfather stopped cooking and changing his shirts, so the hamburger meat in the refrigerator rotted with the crumbs on his breast pocket and then Jimmy's mom sent a present out of season.

I was gonna comfort Jimmy and ask him to put the box back on the high shelf and climb carefully off the steamer trunk Grandmother had brought from the old country when times were bad, but then he said – bless his idiot soul! – that the *empty* box was exactly what he'd wanted and that it verified the success of the mind-messages.

What about the map? I asked.

This is the map, he said.

It's an empty shoebox, I said.

But it's a *shoe*box and it's her shoebox, and so that is a clue that I should begin walking in her shoes to find her.

I called him a fool.

Then he called me a goodfornothing.

So I pushed him.

So he fell and cut his eye on the trunk's corner. If Jimmy hadn't cut his eye then I wouldn't have had to wake up Grandfather. But Jimmy's pouring face blood was staining the rug from the same old country so I had to go into Grandfather's room and calmly explain the situation rather than screaming my head off, which won't accomplish anything.

Of course, I didn't know Jimmy had climbed *inside* the trunk until Grandfather put his suspenders back on and followed me to the situation. He saw the blood and the area rug and empty shoe box. Then he opened the trunk and there was Jimmy, bleeding all over Grandmother's – god rest her

– special-occasion linens. So Grandfather wouldn't have to waste breath, I called Jimmy a damn fool, but he must like to waste his breath because he called to that young man to get out of that trunk right now or hell would pay.

Off the record, how can hell pay if God's got all the rubies and diamonds in heaven and he wouldn't give the devil any diamonds to pawn for money to pay Grandfather?

Grandfather asked if Jimmy had gone deaf. When Jimmy didn't answer, I explained that Jimmy was in his eternal resting place like Grandmother. Jimmy popped his head up and asked how I knew that. I said I must have gotten his mind-message and we laughed and shook hands and Grandfather sat right down on the rug and put his head in his hands and started crying. Tiny water drops ran out of his hands and down his saggy arms and off his elbows onto the blood-stained rug. It looked like his hands were crying.

I like that man very much, so don't say I said he was crying.

Before I could kiss Grandfather's baldy head and put on a pot of coffee so we could discuss this matter like adults, Jimmy saw Grandfather couldn't see and so he leaped out of the trunk – a special-occasion pillowcase wrapped around his head – and ran out the door. Grandfather jumped up like the spry young man he once was and ran after Jimmy, yelling not to run away like your goodfornothing father, which probably made Jimmy think slower and so he scrambled up our dearly beloved Grandmother's morning glories and onto the roof.

Had it not been the hottest day on record and had Grandmother loved roses instead of morning glories, Grandfather woulda gotten control of himself and Jimmy woulda come down shortly.

But Grandfather yelled up that Jimmy better stay up there if he knew what was good for him. Then he went back inside.

Jimmy stood real still up there. I yelled in Grandmother's voice to come down, but he didn't say nothing back. He didn't even look down. I was turning to get the ladder when he screamed. Screamed that he was stuck. I said you certainly are.

No, he hollered, I tried to pick up my foot, but I've melted. To the roof. Call the fire truck, he shouted.

Now, if he hadn't said fire truck, I wouldn't have remembered the purry kitten my mother gave me on my fourth birthday or how when I tried to push it in the park swing, it ran off and scrambled up a tree. Mom called the fire truck, and the firemen brought a ladder taller than the slide. The fireman carried my dangnumb kitten real gentle down the ladder and handed it to my mother. I reached for it, but she didn't give it back. Then the bad man came and my mom and my kitten went to the playhouse and my kitty made the same sound Mom did when the man turned her arm into a broken cassette tape. But my kitty didn't smile. When the man left, I went into the playhouse, but my kitty wasn't there. Mom said the man took it to climb heaven's trees. I said we should call the firemen. Mom said their ladder wasn't tall enough. Then we drove to the Grands' and Grandmother gave me a stuffed animal cat so I cried so Grandmother called me disrespectful so Mom and her went into the guest bedroom. When they came out, Grandmother put me in her lap, pointed at my belly, and said my purry kitten lived inside me now.

I asked her to take it out.

I opened my mouth real wide.

She shook her head.

Then my mother left and hasn't come back.

If I had called the fire truck for Jimmy, the bad man would come and Jimmy would have to climb heaven's roofs or live in my stomach with my kitty and play all the games I want to play with it.

I asked why *he* couldn't send a message to the fireman since he had good reception up there. He said if I weren't a goodfornothing, I'd bring him the big knife from the kitchen drawer.

Seeing as how I'm not what he said, I got the knife.

Seeing as how I was liable to chop his head off if I threw it up to him, I delivered it in person.

Jimmy had sunk into the roof so far I couldn't see his piggy toes. He never cleans the lint out or cuts his toenails. But god's honest, when I couldn't see those toes, I felt bad about ever calling him lizard feet. He said he would cut off his feet, then when the sun went down, he'd pull his feet out of the roof with his mind-waves and then put them back on. It will be my best mind-trick ever, he said, and I agreed because really, it would have been.

I shoulda known he wasn't thinking clearly on account of he never does plus his bleeding head plus the sun. I handed him the knife. Hurry up, I said.

I'm getting up my gumption, he said.

In recollection, we should have waited for him to sink through the roof and out the ceiling into the dining room. But I didn't have recollection then. He kinda bent over and sliced his ankle like Grandfather while shaving. But Grandfather never faints. Jimmy did. Because of do unto others, I sat down next to Jimmy's legs and took up the knife. The world wasn't made in a minute and patience is a virtue I've been working on, so I kept at it and shut my mouth tight and sawed like Grandmother taught me to cut bread without smashing it.

After Jimmy was free, I rolled him down to the gutter Grandfather hoses leaves – and once a dead baby bird – out of every autumn. Then I climbed back down and threw my coverlet over the bushes below just like I'd practised in case of a fire or if Mom came back. Then I got back up there and pushed him off. He fell bull's-eye on the coverlet. When the ambulance men came and strapped Jimmy on the rolling bed, he started screaming that he wished he'd never been born. Grandfather and I just stood there sending mind messages back and forth, but I don't know what they said.

Drift

I was eight years old when I met my mother's kidnapper. My father was in the kitchen making lemonade when Mom called. Her car was in the shop, so he had to pick her up from work at the hotel. She asked if he was there. Of course. Give him the phone, sweetie. Wait. She paused. You know I love you more than anything? Sure, Mom. I handed him the phone as he wiped pulp into the pitcher. When he hung up, he said a busload of church ladies arrived at the motel without a reservation. Chaos.

He put the lemonade in the refrigerator and turned on the TV. We flipped between two movies. One was a horror movie about a motel film camp. The other, a documentary about murder. It was hard to remember which was which.

When the credits rolled, my father called again. Is everything settled? he asked her. He looked at his watch. Then the porch. Then my face. Then his watch. I shrank into the couch. It was past my bedtime. We watched another show. He called again. He said he could drive over and just wait. No, he said, you're not walking home at this hour. Then his voice dropped, and he said her name.

I always thought I'd know my soul mate when I heard my name said like how my father said my mother's name. When my marriage was disintegrating, I told my mother that fate had destined my marriage for failure from the beginning because my husband never said my name right. Right? she asked. After I explained, she said my father's sister died when they were children, and that the ripple in his voice was his fear of people leaving him. I asked why she never told me. He's my husband, she said. His secrets are my secrets.

On his way to the front porch – phone in hand – my father said to go to bed. Every night they sat on the porch drinking lemonade. I always tried to stay awake, but their weaving voices put me to sleep. Once, I crawled down the hallway and crouched by the picture window. They sat close, whispering, touching each other's faces – the green light from the radio curving over their legs. They were always happier out there. When my father was dying, every twilight she wheeled the hospice bed out to the porch.

Maybe I decided to rescue my mother because my father sounded worried, or maybe I heard something in her voice. Sometimes, I think a man spoke on her side of the line. But memory is so pliable. At my high-school reunion, one of my friends said I punched her in the face in kindergarten. I said she must be mistaken. When I told my mother, she laughed and nodded.

I crept down the hallway, ready in case my mother was actually home and the phone call was just an elaborate kidnapping-prevention plan. So I stayed low in case she did one of her usual routines: jumping out of the hall closet and yelling, I'm an attacker – what do you do?

When I made the wrong move, she cried and held me so tight my ribs rubbed.

I was near the bathroom when my father came back inside. I flew to my room and leapt into bed so the kidnapper under my bed couldn't pull me under to where all the missing children were buried.

He went into the kitchen. The refrigerator sucked open. He stirred the lemonade. I imagined him letting go of the spatula. How it kept twirling. He never told us the secret recipe. When searching for his living will, I opened the safety-deposit box and found the recipe written on an index card in his loopy cursive.

The screen door shut.

I made it to the garage on the second attempt.

I removed the noisemakers from my bike and strapped on my kneepads and elbow pads and the yellow vest with orange stripes my mother stuck on like Band-Aids. I carefully moved my bike from the wall of milk cartons my mother had collected since she was eleven. Each pint-sized carton stacked on another. Each carton a missing child's face.

If I ever talked to a stranger, even if the person was nice, Mom drove me home and parked in the garage, headlights spotlighting the smiling faces.

These kids talked to strangers, she'd say. And where are they now?

Dead and rotting, I'd answer.

Every year when I got my school pictures, she glued one to the milk jug in the refrigerator to remind me what could happen. Once, as a joke, I glued her picture to the milk jug. When she saw it, she shook me until my jaw popped.

I wheeled my bike out the side door and wished I could climb in my father's lap and rub my cheek against his beard. I always had a hard time leaving him. He didn't like driving very far, so my mother and I often visited my grandfather alone. As she backed out of our driveway to begin the trip, my father looked so lonely there on the porch. His elbows on his knees. His blue eyes focused on nothing. I knew if I went to him, he'd smile and kiss my forehead, but his eyes would still be the same. He was a sad man. That would have been a better epitaph.

I took the back roads and cut across the field to avoid the main highway. When I got to the motel, I rode behind the building to the dumpster where Mom usually parked. A brown car was there instead. According to one of my mother's stories, once, when she took out the motel trash, she heard a baby cry and saw a girl half-in and half-out of the dumpster. The girl's shoes had fallen off. My mother picked them up. Size seven, she'd say as she told it. My size, she'd say and look at her hands as if she were holding the shoes. Then she'd set the invisible shoes down and continue with how she pulled the baby from the dumpster and lifted it over the edge, down into the girl's outstretched arms. The girl sat down, unsnapped her blouse, and began nursing. When I asked what happened to the girl, my mother shrugged. She gave the same answer: Happily ever after.

On the way around the motel parking lot, I didn't see my mother or the bus from her phone call. A girl with blue hair sat in the lobby in my mother's chair, her feet on the desk, a magazine on her lap. I'd never seen her. She might have known where my mother was, but she could be a kidnapper. Anybody could take me into the forest like in fairy tales or the TV shows where good things never happen except in updates.

Mother recorded all the episodes about missing children. She watched them again and again, pausing when the age-enhanced picture or drawing appeared. She kept a camera in her car so if she ever saw one of the children and couldn't get them in time, she could snap a shot of the kidnapper's license plate. She took many rolls of film and sat by the TV, holding each picture against the screen. Once, she wanted to make fliers with the pictures and post them around town. Father said no. Please, she said. They aren't missing, he said. But I need to know that someone notices the pictures. The kids' parents need to know that if their kid is stolen that someone will see the picture and call instead of not bothering to stop and look. No, Father said.

I set my bike down by the huge yellow signboard that read FREE HBO. CONTINENTAL BREAKFAST. I once thought continental breakfasts had to do with what my grandfather taught me about the world and how it was once one piece and over billions of years, it unlocked and floated apart. He talked about Alexander the Great who warred across a continent because he was a genius and greedy sonofa. Later, men sailed across oceans and into continents that didn't exist before they found them. When the continents heard of each other, they went to war because one continent remembered being part of the whole and fought to make the other continent remember.

I used this metaphor when explaining divorce to my daughter. I sat her in front of a globe. I pointed. I clasped my hands. Then I slowly pulled my fingers apart. My husband sat by, waiting to say that divorce happens when two people don't love each other anymore. No, I said. It's when two people don't love each other in the *same* way. No, he said. There's no more love. I threw the globe at his head.

If I looked through the vacation albums while Grandfather was around, he asked if I knew the amazing story of Shawnee Forest's creation. I always said no. His eyes got big, and his right arm became a glacier and his left arm, Illinois. The glacier arm slid down the Illinois arm, melting and making all the hills and flat places and unrolling his sleeve as it went. Isn't that amazing, he'd say, and I'd nod. Then he'd give me a jar of pennies and go to the attic to paint landscapes.

The first page of all my grandparents' vacation albums is a picture of Mom in front of the Shawnee cabin. She's five. She smiles. She's twelve. She doesn't. She's sixteen. She squints. She's twenty. She stares off. Then Father's with her and they're laughing. Then I'm in his arms, and she's trying to wipe my face. Then Father's in a wheelchair and Mom's in his lap, my husband and pregnant me behind them.

Once, I found a picture of Mom as a little girl in a turquoise bathing suit. She's crying on a large rock. When I showed it to her, she asked if I remembered the night I met the man at the motel. The little girl she once was had climbed the rock to get away from him. When she got up there, she couldn't get down. The man found her and laughed, snapping picture after picture, the film advancing frame by frame, the sound echoing throughout the canyon.

For a long time, I didn't connect her turquoise swimsuit to the bedtime story that I still have the nightmares from. I told it to my daughter after I took her to the circus and she saw a clown with balloons, let go of my hand, and ran off. I took her straight home, bringing back to life the story of the mother who left her daughter at the park swimming pool. The little girl stood at the fence waiting for her mom to return. A man walked up and offered her a peppermint pattie. Said her mother got a flat tire and asked him to come get her. The little girl walked around the fence and followed him. She trusted everyone, my mother would say. She didn't know. She just didn't know.

What happened to the little girl? I'd ask. Did she escape? I don't know, baby, she said. I don't know.

When my daughter told my husband the story, he stormed into our bedroom and we had my mother and father's argument. But instead of retreating to the bathroom like my mother, I made us sit in the car, the windows up so our daughter couldn't hear him yell the past is the past so leave it there while I yelled that history does repeat, and he said he wasn't that man, and I took my mother's voice and said I can't help it! Instead of holding me and saying everything's okay then leading me to the porch swing, he got in his car and drove off. When my daughter marries, she'll have a new place for arguments so her children can't hear.

When we separated, I used the money for our tenth-anniversary vacation and had a porch added to the house. He left his girlfriend, whom I pretended didn't exist, long enough to have an anniversary picnic on the new porch. We admired the jasmine, how large it had grown since our daughter was in diapers. I thought about making love to him right there, our heads on the doormat. But then he asked why I blew the money on a porch when he always wanted a swimming pool.

The real estate agent said the porch sealed the deal for the new owners.

Mom had said that if I were ever kidnapped to a motel to watch the lock because kidnappers get sloppy. She said not to hide because I could be found. Run and scream are the best bets. I ran into the motel stairwell lit red by the Coke machine. With my back against the stair railing, I walked up to the balcony. I tested doorknobs in case she left one open as a sign.

I imagined my father calling the motel and the blue-haired girl answering instead of Mom. He drops the phone and goes into my bedroom. I'm not there. He searches for the car keys.

One of the doors finally opened. A light was on above the table by the window, but no one was inside. I sat on the table and looked out onto the parking lot. Nothing happened. I jumped from bed to bed then turned on the TV. The next thing I remember is the door opening. Laughter. Because I was half-in and half-out of a dream, I thought the blue-haired girl was shaking me awake. But my eyes opened to my mother.

She leaned over me, her blouse gaping open, the curve of breast. The third button hole was safety-pinned. She often left safety pins on the bathroom sink where they rusted, leaving orange outlines on the porcelain.

Where's your father? she said.

A man sat at the table by the window. He was older. Handsome. He tapped his cigarette ashes into a Coke can.

This is a non-smoking room, I said.

He laughed and tapped his cigarette again, ashes fizzling in what liquid was left.

I wondered why she hadn't explained the policy. How non-smokers complained until they got a discount or another room.

She looked at me. Then at the man. Then at my father across town on the porch, his hunched figure backlit by the picture window.

You shouldn't be here, she said and brushed my bangs to the side of my face, even though they weren't long enough to be in my eyes. She never did that.

The man smiled when I looked at him. His smile hurt. He shook another cigarette from his pack.

I thought you didn't want children, he said and winked at my mother like he had a bad secret. I saw the same look on my daughter's face when she reported my husband was remarrying. I worried how he'd tell his new wife my secrets. How they'd laugh over them in bed. How she'd tell him her secrets, and eventually, they'd replace mine.

I narrowed my eyes at the man. Smoke hovered in the green lampshade above his head.

You take after your mother when she was about your age, he said.

Her fingers dug into my wrist.

I can't believe you, she said.

He shrugged. Snapped a match. Come now, he said.

Don't talk to her, she said.

I prayed her tears would hold off because I always cried when she did, which was often because there's always another milk carton, another episode of age-enhanced faces.

We had a good time, he said. You didn't want to go home.

She covered her mouth and began to shrink until she was my age and buckled into a passenger seat and the story that surrounds every swimming pool I've ever seen.

I was ten and a half, she said, her voice a mouse flinging a trap around.

He tilted his head, as if she really were a child. I remember, he said. Your parents were neither dead nor divorced.

The green light stared between them.

Then my father's voice broke everything. Our names flew across the parking lot and over the balcony.

The man looked at Mom. This must be the good man you'd marry.

My mother began to cry. Harder than at my wedding or when my daughter was in intensive care or when my father was diagnosed.

The motel shuddered with the force of my father on the stairs.

She gasped and hugged herself. She curled on the bed, her forehead against her knees.

My father yelled our names and pounded on every door. His face was red when it appeared in the window. The man turned and waved at him. My father pushed and pulled at the door. My mother's high heels fell off her feet. I picked them up. Size seven. My father began screaming I'll kill you, I'll kill you. I didn't know who he meant, but his eyes said all of us. I held my mother. His footsteps retreated.

My grandfather walked in and stood on a chair, his arm making a forest.

I whispered that I loved her and everything would be okay while my daughter crawled into a corner and began spinning a globe.

Everything will be okay, Mommy, I said, having no idea if I was right or what to say to my ex-husband in the bathroom as my water broke.

But I couldn't stop saying it's okay to my mother on a rock in the middle of the motel room as all the missing children rose from under the bed and floated through the room, laughing at my father who returns to the window again and again with my mother's camera. He presses the button, and we all light up then disappear. I count the flashes.

Stay

Mother and I spend the year of cancer in a campground. We sit in lawn chairs. It is October. Everyone is gone. The parked campers are empty and waiting for summer.

We hold hands and I trace her soft veins. She traces mine. She closes her eyes and hums tunes once written in player-piano Braille.

This morning she pulled out the tin can, the only thing she brought from home besides her nightgowns. The home sold to pay for the treatments she's stopped. The leftover money now for a parking space and groceries.

Our hair is rolled in the wire curlers.

I ask how much longer should we wear these?

She says until we go to bed because we didn't wet our hair. If you don't roll wet hair, the curls don't stay as well. Then she smiles and loops a loose lock of my hair around her finger.

Remember when I did this when you were a little girl?

I nod.

She keeps her finger there a second longer then lets go.

The couple who own the place wave between their office and house.

We eat lunch, we eat dinner, we play double solitaire on the picnic bench by the in-ground swimming pool empty of water. Mother wins every hand.

We go to bed. We say I love you.

When I was small, Mom danced in the backyard. She'd wind up the player piano in the screened-in porch. I would stand on the windowsill ledge when I was supposed to be watching keys instead of a woman jumping over croquet hoops. Watching to be sure the music didn't stop. She was very famous. Now she's not. That is the way with fame and cancer.

I awake to the camper door. I press my forehead to the

screen window.

Mother walks beneath the orange security lights in her nightgown. Moths flutter. The vending machine between the restrooms pinkens through the fabric. Her breasts are heavy, two anchors. Her back is to me so I can't see the line that plods past her navel. She was gutted and seamed back together before I found her and bought the house.

She fills the tin can at the water fountain. Then she unbuttons her nightgown. Lifts it over her wire-curled head. Her body is an overripe pear.

She hunches in front of the water fountain. She balls up the nightgown, dunks it in the tin. The screen's imprinting my nose. I should run barefoot down the gravel and take the can from her. I should scoop her up in a blanket and carry her back to her childhood. I'll set her on that sidewalk and say draw. Draw, Eloise Lynn. Draw the woman you will be, but leave out the breasts. The belly. Only two arms and two legs to dance. Then the cancer won't fish for pears.

126

And Yet

There are times on an elevator when a person can imagine that, rather than going down, the elevator is going up, just like the times when spring looks like fall, or winter like summer, and someone in November can imagine the next month is May. But convincing oneself of May during November and *staying* convinced are two different matters, maybe as different as life and death or as similar – in the way that it's a compliment to say that the child's corpse in the coffin looks at peace.

Perhaps the reason the person even imagines that the next month is May instead of December derives from a reason hidden from the person. Perhaps the person imagines this because of escapist coping mechanisms. We're told that we can never know. And so, instead of worrying about that inability to know, we agree that above all, a person's mood is as prone to manipulation as the spots on the moon that can become the skull-hollow shadows of the man who resides there.

This shifting from what we're supposed to know and what we'd like to fancy, defined as imagination in elementary school and madness after, is why our lady in the hospital elevator reviles calendars and mentally squirms every time she must consult the planner in her wallet for when she can make it here to visit her son.

The planner where – after the doctor told her – she (against her better judgment) wrote the date of her son's expected death (just as she had marked his due date when she learned she was pregnant). Just like she knows today she must finally tell him he's dying, she knows-but-does-not-want-to-know that she will eventually consult the planner to confirm when in the afternoon she must drive to the funeral home and pick out the casket, when this or that relative's plane will land, and when the visitation or showing, as some call it, will happen.

Her revulsion to calendars has not spun into some obsessive

quirk; she simply has her thoughts about calendars, and if the next person to step into the elevator asked her what those thoughts were, she'd simply say, Calendars make it hard to live one day at a time. So there, her nod would say.

Calendars heckle her belief, rather her *need* to believe, that tomorrow might not happen if she does not deal with today. Because of calendars, May following November is splendid fantasy or corner-rocking madness. And because she is tired and her son is dying and she is, on the most basic level, irritated at herself for buying her first pack of cigarettes in almost eight years, the fact of calendars receives all her helplessness disguised as wrath. Calendars. Damn them. Bradbury should have written a book about burning calendars instead of books.

If every calendar turned into ashes in a cup, she could keep imagining that the elevator she stands in, her hand lightly resting on the railing welded to its wall, is going in the opposite direction of the floor number she pushed.

The seventh floor is lined with rooms full of dying children, and the rooms are lined with their hospital beds like any collection that's being watched. Seven years ago, one of the children slid from the body of the lady who now stands in the moving elevator, her eyes averted from the glowing orange number in the row of unlit numbers, the number that is two numbers above the maternity floor that death seems to touch just a little more lightly, a little more accidentally, than the rest.

Her seven-year-old baby has not yet told her he knows he's dying. He *will* tell her because there are matters to be dealt with, for example, he wants to die in his own bed, on his own pillowcase patterned with baseball players mid-pitch and batters sliding into home. But he will never tell her that he knows she already knew but hadn't told him, and he will never tell her that he knew about his dying for a while but waited to tell her because of knowing she can cope only one

128

day at a time.

(One day at a time, she always says – we'll get through this one day at a time – a phrase she will use without question her whole life, a phrase as useful and helpful as the cigarette that shouldn't but does make the current events of her life come into slightly clearer focus.)

She can cope with filling her son's little hospital pitcher with water from the bathroom, she can cope with reading him the cards from his friends and classmates and her friends and their church friends and so on. She can cope with the empathy of strangers because, like her ex-husband says, the empathy of strangers is usually sympathy standing on pity's shoulders beneath a trench coat disguised as empathy. She can cope with *that*, but she cannot cope with empathy from her son because she is the mother, after all, and so empathy is her job, in the same way that filling his pitcher with water and reading him greeting cards and trying not to ask him too often how he feels is her job.

And he will not knowingly take that job away from her because that would make her feel like a bad mother, if not for those reasons then because she'll feel like he kept a secret from her that should not have been a secret, and that would make her say nice things through sharp teeth just like the times she found out he had a super good time with his father during a weekend visit. When she feels like a bad mother, she becomes a different mother, and he does not want a different mother just like he doesn't want to die next to a window that does not open and does not overlook his backyard and the sturdy tree where his tire swing hangs.

Realizing his mother's tendencies and allowing for them does not make the boy a sage or confirm that he has an old soul. And though the poem inside the pamphlet at his funeral will say he was an angel who came to visit earth for seven years before God missed him and greedily called him back to the moon or wherever God sits, like a nurse, to watch the current events, the boy *is not* an angel and to say this to his mother while she sobs into her knuckles by his grave or by his empty tire swing is only to make her feel as though she is the greedy one for not wanting him to vanish and that her grief is inhuman rather than basic and honest, a cigarette during a tornado or a glance held away from the floor an elevator travels toward.

He is a boy who knows about his mother's tendencies and shapes his words to them because he remembers the ordinary round of pitch and catch in the backyard when his father told him he planned to move out. His father told him not to say anything to his mother, though, because he hadn't told her yet. When the boy spoke, he didn't ask his father why he was leaving but why he hadn't told her yet, and his father said, You'll see – it's kind of like breaking in a mitt.

After many days of watching his mother as he never had, he realized she somehow already knew about the ensuing separation by the way she kissed his father a second longer than usual, how her voice was a little higher during arguments and a little lower when she said sweet dreams. Then he woke up in the night to the car reversing out of the driveway and into the street, headlights sweeping across his room, lighting up the chalkboard that covered one wall, the streetlight illuminating the car's interior for a second. His mother was smiling. He couldn't see his father's face, but he imagined it held an expression similar to that day tossing the ball in the backyard.

While his parents drove up and down country roads, he crept around the unlit house, searching with his hands and memory for a place to hide. This time he was not hiding from the creature ready to reach out and do whatever horrible things creatures do to children who don't wake up in time from nightmares or who don't pull their feet far enough away from the edge of the bed.

As he edged around his father's recliner and brushed up

against the coat rack, what caused the fright that clutched at his throat and coursed through him like hot pee when he had the flu and what he searched to hide from was the anticipation of the new mother who would return that night inside the same old car in his old mother's body beside the same old father.

After his father cut the engine and reached – out of habit – across her trembling breast to push her door open, she, this new mother, would untangle the old mother's feet from the floorboard and walk into the house on the old mother's zombified legs, her face a zombie's, and when she took him into her arms, her arms would tighten just a bit more, while her new voice – which was his old mother's zombified voice – said that she still loves him and that Daddy still loves him and everything will be alright, we'll just take this one day at a time.

He knew the new mother would make the old mother say this because a couple of his friends had reported their parents saying the same thing and that's what the actors pretending to be divorcing parents always said in G-rated movies.

He did crawl up under the footstool where he often balled up when his father watched scary movies in which parents might divorce but the actors didn't make speeches about it because there were worse things to talk about – the clown that fills sinks with blood or the woman who drowns any children who wander down to the river at night – but like always, his legs cramped after a while, so he backed out and returned (like the car that held his parents) to his bedroom, shutting the door as his old mother had, tucking himself into bed as she had, and then began waiting for what he still wanted to hide from.

And all that he had imagined came true except that while the new mother's zombie arms enclosed him, he reached out and patted her hair and said, S'okay, Mom, we'll get through this one day at a time and then one day it won't be so bad just like when I busted my knee open, right? And when he said that, she pulled back, shaking her head in disbelief at not only his lack of tears but also how goddamn similar he was to the man who was moving out in the morning. Then her face changed and she appeared to her son not like the old mom or new mom but the mom from the pictures in the floral albums in the hall closet who smiled with dark circles under her eyes as she held a baby she said was him not so long ago or far away. One day at a time, she repeated then realized she was repeating herself because he had learned that assurance from her.

Then she thought of their first family car trip when he was three years old, how he'd called out from the back seat, Are we there yet? and she and her husband looked at each other and busted up because they certainly hadn't taught him that.

She let out a giggle and said to her son, who still cupped his small hand around the curve of her skull, One day at a time. Well, are we there yet? And they chuckled together, not as adult and child, but as two old friends meeting after many years and falling back into rhythm.

Right now, a lady in an elevator rages at calendars and tries to forget the elevator's direction – to the seventh floor or to the first floor that will take her just outside the swooshing doors where she can shake out a cigarette and contemplate how she's supposed to tell her baby he's dying – while a boy, not a prophet but a human who has lived for seven years, sits in a hospital bed thinking about how nice it will be to get into his mother's car and drive home to his bedroom.

He knows the doctors told her he's dying, but she just needs a little more time to break in the idea – like a baseball mitt, yeah, that's something he'll do when he gets home, play a little solitaire catch in bed. Then, once the idea's broken in enough, he can tell her he knows the score and then they'll get in the car – just like his parents got in a car married then returned separated an hour later – and he can die with his regular mom instead of the hospital mom who reads all those cheesy cards and is always running off with his water pitcher that just makes him fill the bag of pee next to his bed faster.

Then he can just be himself again and enjoy the rest of his own car ride. And when the car ride is over, well, what a relief it will be to finally get there and meet that silly man in the moon. Besides, he gets carsick pretty easily. Carsick. He giggles to himself and then thinks about how his buddies would bust a gut at his joke and that makes the giggle too big to hold in.

The girl in the bed beside his turns her pale face to him and asks what's funny and he tells her and she giggles and the girl next to her asks what's so damn funny, and so after giggling about the word damn, they tell that girl and the girl says, Well, are we there yet? and that really sets them off and soon the whole roomful of kids are repeating are we there yet?! and their laughter fills the room and some kick their beds or slap their foreheads like their parents did before they became hospital parents. This one's a real side-splitter and soon the nurses hear the children and hurry in looking around for the clown that tells the same G-movie jokes every time and isn't scheduled until later that afternoon.

But there isn't a clown and the nurses' mouths drop open because first they think all the kids are going into hysterical seizures, and so, of course, to the kids, that's absolutely hee-lair-ee-us because the nurses never make those faces and one child points at a nurse and says it looks like the grinning teddy bears on her smock are falling out of her mouth, and it really does, and so the laughter turns into the happiest tornado and if any of the nurses think this can be controlled or stopped, they are wrong.

Two Ravens Press is the most northerly literary publisher in the UK, operating from a six-acre working croft on a sea-loch in the north-west Highlands of Scotland. We publish cutting-edge and innovative contemporary fiction, non-fiction and poetry.

Visit our website for comprehensive information on all of our books and authors – and for much more:

- browse all Two Ravens Press books by category or by author, and purchase them online, post & packing-free (in the UK, and for a small fee overseas)

- there is a separate page for each book, including summaries, extracts and reviews, and author interviews, biographies and photographs

- read our daily blog about life as a small literary publisher in the middle of nowhere – or the centre of the universe, depending on your perspective – with a few anecdotes about life down on the croft thrown in. Includes regular and irregular columns by guest writers – Two Ravens Press authors and others.

www.tworavenspress.com